What The Eyes Don't See (Paranormal)

Jasmins Johnston

Copyright © 2024 by Jasmins Johnston

All rights reserved.

No portion of this book may be reproduced in any form without written permission from the publisher or author, except as permitted by U.S. copyright law.

Contents

1. Chapter 1 — 1
2. Chapter 2 — 8
3. Chapter 3 — 17
4. Chapter 4 — 23
5. Chapter 5 — 29
6. Chapter 6 — 37
7. Chapter 7 — 42
8. Chapter 8 — 47
9. Chapter 9 — 53
10. Chapter 10 — 59
11. Chapter 11 — 62
12. Chapter 12 — 68
13. Chapter 13 — 76
14. Chapter 14 — 84

15. Chapter 15 88

Chapter 1

In that glass-walled conference room, three pairs of eyes were riveted to the large monitor on the wall. There was another pair of eyes, carefully scrutinizing the other three. As the video began to play, this young man, Anay Ghosh, wheeled his swivel chair back by a few inches. His intention was to get to a suitable vantage point to observe the others. And as each frame of the clip played, that was exactly what he did. Observe.

The older man in the group seemed to be enthusiastic. He was Mr Sen, the client who had to be impressed for the deal. The signs were positive. Sen peered at the faces of the characters in the video with narrowed eyes; always a good indication of engrossment.

His younger colleague did not seem so impressed, though. He watched with the disapproving glare of a hawk, eager to point out a mistake. He took silent notes. His mental cogwheels seemed to turn so furiously that it caused some worry in the observer. But then the observer knew an important dynamic—the younger disapproving colleague was a junior. All his diligence in nitpicking flaws in the clip weren't aimed at any quest for creative analysis. They were only to earn brownie points with his boss.

Anay brushed the younger associate aside. He did not matter.

The third pair of eyes was Anay's boss, Salil Jani, the creative director of the company. He, of course, mattered. Prospective clients like Sen would come and go, but the boss had to be kept happy always. And he seemed to be! Anay did a little jig in his mind when his boss swayed his head in tune with the final jingle.

"Excellent work, if I say so myself," said Salil, practically beaming at his protégé. "Didn't I tell you, Mr Sen, that our Anay is the best?"

Anay purred like a well-fed kitten. For him, the stakes were higher than anyone else in the room.

Sen's associate, the super eager junior, leaned forward. "Yes, no doubt it's a brilliant ad for our cat food product, but I think there are not enough cats in the ad. Did you not think so too, sir?"

Sen frowned. It was the beginning of a thought, implanted in his head by his junior. An associate who wasn't supposed to matter. As Anay held his breath, Sen made a slight nod. "Come to think of it, there should be more cats. It's a cat food commercial, after all!"

Salil's face lost color. His smug smile vanished. Somewhere in the back of his mind, he could see the client closing this meeting too without arriving at a decision. He could see another week of harrowing brainstorming and then the work that would follow—rewriting the script, getting the actors, reshooting the ad. He balked at the further expense that would entail; they had already overshot the development fee. "Of course, Mr Sen. If that's your concern, it must be addressed," he said. "What do you say to that, Anay?"

Anay, who had his arms folded until now, unfolded them and assumed the stance of a person who had a confident reply to a puzzling conundrum. "I agree, Salil sir, that is a justified question!" he said with the smile intact on his face. "It is kind of Milind to point it out, for it gives me a chance to explain my position." It was a calculated trick. Address the junior by his first name so that he feels important. Concur with him so that he feels validated and can go back and brag to his colleagues about his valuable contribution to the meeting. But don't append his name with 'sir' to show that he's just an equal. "So, you see, we arrived at this decision to have only three cats in the ad after much thought. We focused on the owners of the cats rather than the cats themselves. The ad follows the issues of the cat-owners and addresses them in a funny way, as you might have observed. The worry when there's no cat food in the house, the cat food is not nutritious enough, where to go to get it... all these are common pet-owner questions. And that is what our ad answers instead of showing cutesy cats in every frame, which every mediocre ad-maker will do, because that's the first thought that pops in the head."

"But I think..." Milind began.

"No, it's fine!" Sen cut in. "I buy this young man's explanation. It's right. We have been showing cute cat faces in all our ads so far. Our customers are bored of those ads. We wanted a new approach and hence we came to Changemakers. Well, it's done. I am convinced. Salil, you can go ahead and draft your agreement. You have our business."

Salil could not contain his happiness. He stood up as Sen and his junior stood and shook hands with him with the most profuse of curtsies. Anay stood up too, and he ensured to nod and smile at the junior when shaking hands with him. In this business, one could not afford any hard feelings.

When the clients left, Salil turned to Anay. "Well, you did it!" He patted Anay on the back, a tad too hard. "And now, since you have proven yourself, let's see what I can do about giving you the Senior Creative Team Leader position."

Anay had no words. For once, the eloquent speaker and convincer in him was speechless. He followed his boss out of the conference room with a spring in his step.

When he reached outside, he was stopped by a peon in the blue company uniform. He had an empty tray in his hand, and came up to Anay, full of purpose. "Is the meeting over, Anay sir?" he asked.

Anay nodded.

"You look happy, sir! Good news?"

"Yes, Sudhir, the deal is ours! Wait for Salil sir to announce a party!"

The peon cracked a smile. "Well, that's nice. Let me clean up the conference room. Next time, I will arrange the bigger conference room so that all five of you can sit comfortably."

Anay grunted an assent. And then that word caught his attention. "Five? There were only four of us."

The peon frowned. He thought a bit and then shook his head. "Why are you joking, sir? I saw five of you. Two suits from that cat company, Salil sir, you, and that man standing behind you."

"Man standing behind me? There was no one standing behind me."

The peon laughed. "Nice joke, sir. Then whom did I bring the fifth tea for? A ghost?"

Anay looked back into the conference room. There were indeed five cups. Surely it was some kind of confusion.

Or even a practical joke.

"Very funny, Sudhir! Go easy on those specially hand-rolled cigarettes and you'll be fine!" Anay laughed and left.

The Bandana was the local watering hole, the hippest place in town for young nightcrawlers. It was but understood that Anay would hang out there, for he was at least at Changemakers the flavor of the season. The place, with its retro music so loud that you could not do anything but drink and lip-read the people with you, was currently in the throes of a wild Friday night. The lights had been dimmed more than usual and strange neon glows adorned the walls that sported portraits of Oscar and Grammy-winning cult pop icons of the 80s and 90s. It was the place to be!

Anay was with his usual coterie. It included Kautuk and Vishwa from commercials and Renee from HR. They had all met at Changemakers, their common bond being that they had all been recruited in the same financial year three years ago, albeit in different departments. Anay's was, of course, creative. Presently, Vishwa was busy hitting on Renee—a routine that everyone was fast getting sick of, for Renee was either blind or loved the process of being hit on rather than the person who did the hitting on—while Kautuk, as usual, was looking for life's little philosophies in his tall tumbler of lager.

"Just like this froth," Kautuk said with a hiccup, "our lives, I mean, just like the froth on this beer. If you don't glug it down soon, you won't enjoy any of it."

"What did you say?" Anay screamed over the Duran Duran song. But, of course, he had heard him loud and clear. This was only his way to ward off any further exposition of Kautuk's philosophy for the evening.

"I said—"

"But didn't Anay set the conference room on fire today!" Renee chimed in, almost flirtatiously. "I should have been there. I heard you gave some kind of brilliant monologue to convince the client. It would have been such fun to see Salil having a near orgasm..."

"Baby, you say such things and make me so hot!" Vishwa said with a moaning sound and put his arm around her.

"You need to cool down then," Renee retorted. "Why don't you focus on your beer?"

Anay stopped the waiter and ordered another round of chicken pops. He didn't need to ask the others before placing the order. They had been coming here for six months now, every weekend, and this evening he was footing the bill anyway. He leaned forward and said, "So anyway thanks, Renee, for setting me up in that apartment. It's a nice one. Good view of the sea."

"My plez, buddy!" Renee said, absentmindedly (or consciously?) strumming her fingers on Vishwa's arm. "Dad just had to talk to his real estate agent buddy and you got the house. It isn't easy for singles to get apartments in Mumbai otherwise, whether boys or girls. And you've got it in this prime building in happening Versova."

"Yeah, I tell you, it could not have been better."

"Why did you never fix me up in an apartment, sweets?" Vishwa asked.

"Because I like where you stay!"

"I share a room with my brothers in my parents' house."

"Isn't that great?"

Vishwa took a large sip of the beer trying to understand what that meant.

Kautuk shook things up with another of his nuggets, "An apartment is just a shell that we create around ourselves."

"Fucking shit, buddy!" Vishwa retorted. "Where do you stay then?"

"In an apartment. That's what I am saying. It's our compulsion. We humans cannot not stay in a house, can we?"

Anay pushed the chair back and stood up. Gesturing at the others, he made a beeline to the far end of the pub. He entered the men's room, which was surprisingly empty for this time on a Friday evening.

The music cut off as soon as the door swung close, and he welcomed that silent pause. Walking up to a stall, he looked up at the ceiling and unzipped. As the hastily drowned beer coursed out of his aching bladder, he had a deep sense of comfort that culminated in a sigh.

The deed done, he walked to the sink and let the water do its job on his hands, while he checked himself out in the swanky mirror. Despite those sunken work-worn eyes and the dazed pub expression, he was pleased with himself. Everything was right about his face; he had always known that. That broad forehead with the deep-set wide eyes, the long straight nose with its sharp tip, the square jaw that made cover-page models out of mere men, and the well-groomed stubble on his narrow chin—he had always been grateful for his looks. Even that skin of his face, which had never seen a single freckle in his teenage was still supple. There was so much he had to thank!

He stooped and splashed water on his precious face. The coolness of it transported him into a divine place, and he splashed more of it. This time he winced a bit, for some of the water went into his eyes.

Blinking, he tried to reach the paper towels on the wall.

He was still blinking away the prickling water in his eyes when he saw a figure standing behind him in the mirror—a black shadowy figure with many arm-like projections waving all around it, the head covered with a conical hood. In that brief flash, which was no longer than a subliminal frame inserted in a movie clip, the thing looked like some kind of giant octopus.

What the fuck was that? Was it something he had seen in a movie suddenly playing on his mind?

All of a sudden, he felt colder than on the peak of a wintry night. Quickly, he turned. But only the polished white tiles of the restroom shone back at him.

Chapter 2

Anay stepped out of the men's room with a frown, cursing himself for working so hard. It was making him see things that he shouldn't. His slapped his cheek to bring himself back to alertness and blinked several times. The music was soon upon him, and this time it was Chumbawamba tub-thumping in all their raucous glory. The good thing was that it drove away all bizarre thoughts from his head.

He was making his way back to his booth in this particular frame of mind, which was when he saw her.

Her!

His feet stopped of their own volition. Only the broadest of smiles grew on his face. Forgetting everything about everything else, his steps turned in the direction of the girl he had spotted, and in four quick steps, he was at her table, overlooking her as she was engaged in deep conversation with a friend.

It took him just a moment to recall her name—in fact, he had never forgotten it—and then he called out, "Shanaya!"

The girl whirled in her seat. "Oh, my gosh! Is that you, Anay? Anay, really?"

She stood up at once, and he could not stop smiling. She still smelled of lavender talc like all those years ago. All of a sudden, nothing mattered. The music, the cacophony around them, the waiters running about, the friends that they had come with. Everything ceased to exist.

"It has been so many years! Fourteen years? Fifteen?" Anay said, calculating in his mind. "You have hardly changed!"

"But you have! You are a man now. Oh, that came out wrong. You know what I mean."

"I do!" He laughed. And then they both laughed again.

"Come, let's sit at that table for a while..." she proposed. As if by some kind of enchantment, there was suddenly an empty table at the far end of the busy pub.

"But your friend..."

"Gina won't mind. Just give me a minute and I'll join you."

Anay could not quell the thoughts in his mind. All these wonderful things happening in his life one after the other—getting the apartment, getting the deal, and now meeting the girl who he had his first crush on—if there was something like living the dream, this was it. Shanaya Gupta! He still remembered how besotted he had been with her in tenth grade. In class, she used to sit three rows ahead of him, looking just as lovely as she did now. Their paths crossed on several occasions. Both were brilliant at all three things that mattered in school—academics, art, and sport—and they were often teamed up in interschool competitions. Those spells were both exciting and torturous to the hormonal Anay. He was so close to her but didn't have the guts to speak out his heart. All he did was to fantasize about her not just in his bed at nights and during long reprieves in the bathroom, but also when he was with her. And then there was that one occasion—that one single occasion—when they kissed.

They had been visiting another school for the science exhibition. There were four of them, but all that mattered to him was that she was in the team. They had had a spectacular win and amidst all the rejoicing, when the teams were waiting for the school bus to arrive to take them home, Anay and Shanaya fell back. As they walked that long corridor of the host school, their fingers grazed each other. She looked at him. There was a peculiar expression on her face. He knew she was ready. His brain stopped functioning and instinct took over. He held her hand and she yielded. The next moment, he placed his lips on hers and gave vent to his passions.

It was their first kiss, but it did not seem like that to him, for he had played it out in his mind for months. If their friends had not come looking for them, goodness knows what else might have happened.

"Hi!" Shanaya said as she hopped on the seat across him. "Deep in thought?"

Anay smiled uneasily. Trying to hide his embarrassment, he said, "Just these thoughts all came flooding back... of our school days."

"They couldn't have been better," she said casually. "But it's so good to meet you, ya! Tell me about yourself. When did you move to Mumbai? What are you doing here?"

The next ten minutes, he updated her about himself. Then she did the same. He did not know how much he retained of it, though. All he could do was stare at her face. It was still so... so girl-like!

"So, who are you here with?" she asked.

"Huh, what?"

"Hey, snap out of your dreaming! I asked you who have you come with..."

"J-just friends..." Anay said. "They are sitting there at that table." He pointed to them. Renee looked back. They had noticed him sitting with a girl and let him be alone.

"She's cute, ya!" Shanaya said, indicating Renee. "Girlfriend?"

"Oh, of course not..." Anay said, a tad too strongly. "I am as single as they come."

"Why?"

"Why?"

"I can't believe you are single. A romantic guy like you..."

Anay blushed. "What about you?"

"You see that sad girl sitting at that table sipping a margarita there alone?" Shanaya pointed. "Well, Gina is my only friend here in Mumbai. That's all."

"So, single you too..." Anay said, a grin sporting his face.

"Uh-huh..."

"You come here often?"

"No... first time."

"Well, you can, you know," Anay said. "I do... and if you feel like, you can sit with us too. We are all lonely hearts here. Let's be lonely together."

"Done!" she said.

For the rest of the evening, they sat with each other. They laughed and slapped each other's arms playfully and decided on a combined dinner order. When that was done, Shanaya said, almost heavily, "It has been such a lovely evening, Anay. Imagine bumping into you like this! Some things, as they say, are meant to happen. But now I have to go. Our residential colony is a bit strict, you see? Gina and I are roomies, and that's how we got the apartment, otherwise who rents out apartments to a single girl?"

Anay didn't want the evening to end. "Let's keep in touch?"

"Of course!" she said and then she entered her number on his phone.

They were outside The Bandana now, Anay and his friends, waiting for their respective cabs. Anay was in a sort of a trance. Was this really happening? He had never really stopped thinking of Shanaya for all these years, and now she was here, practically dropped into his lap.

Kautuk came running. "Thank my lucky stars you guys didn't leave."

"How can we leave without you?" Anay asked. He was standing on the curb while Vishwa and Renee were at a distance, their bodies practically rubbing into each other behind a closed newspaper stall.

Kautuk sighed. "I know you won't. But you know... Vishwa and Renee cannot think of anything but each other, and you have a million things to think about. Easy to forget a stooge like me!"

"Shut up!" Anay laughed. "Where were you?"

Kautuk raised his little finger. "Loo!" Then seeing the lingering smile on Anay's face, he asked, "So, who was she?"

Anay turned alive at that question. "School friend, man!" he said with a distant longing.

"Ah, I see. Childhood friend. The special kind!"

Anay smiled. She was indeed special.

Kautuk took a heavy drag of the cigarette he had lit and blew a smoke ring in the air. Looking at it float away almost meditatively, he said, "The past."

"What does that mean?" Anay asked.

"It's interesting, isn't it? The past? And the way it comes back all of a sudden, as if it to remind us that we haven't moved at all?"

Anay zoned out. It was philosophical Kautuk time again.

He patted Kautuk on his shoulders. The guy was almost doddering on his feet. Though Anay had paid the bill, he had kept no count of how much lager had been ordered. A white cab came up and stopped next to them. "My ride's here," Anay said. "And there's yours too. Call those two lovebirds."

Renee and Vishwa came up. A strange quirk of fate was that, due to the directions of their houses, Renee and Anay shared a cab and Vishwa and Kautuk shared another. Anay got into the cab and waited for Renee to say goodbye to Vishwa with a wet, sloppy kiss. Anay then allowed Renee to get in and then stepped into the cab after her. They watched the other cab drive away in silence.

Then, as their cab started, Renee looked at Anay, wiped Vishwa's saliva off her mouth, and smiled. It was the smile of two people that shared a big secret. "Finally, he's gone!" she said with a sigh. "Oh, I thought he'd never go. He was extra horny today, the poor sucker."

Anay kept his hand on Renee's leg and gently squeezed it. "You should tell him," he said.

"No, man. You know Vishwa. He's too thick to take a hint," said Renee. "But he's got a good heart. I still don't know how I'll tell him."

"You must."

Renee slid closer to Anay. "You know it will break up our group. We have such a good thing going. What's the need to make an announcement?"

Anay relaxed in his seat. He let his hand graze her soft thigh and ride up till as far as he wanted it to. She did not resist. Instead she said with a dried-up throat, "But you know I don't feel for him like I do for you, Anay. I cannot wait till I tell him."

"Me neither," he said and slid his finger under the soft fabric of her panties and felt the tenderness of her vagina. She spread her legs as she let out her first moan. That was where he lost it. To add to it, she brought her hand to his crotch and found his bulge and grabbed hold of it.

Amidst heavy breathing, Anay urged the driver to go as slow as he could and bill extra if he wanted. Then he leaned in and placed his lips on Renee's. He shut his eyes and felt the pulpy warmth of her tongue inside his mouth.

But just as he was surrendering himself to that moment of stolen passion, Anay's mind conjured another face. It happened with the rapidity of a clap of lightning on a stormy night. And that face was of Shanaya. He thought he was back in that lonely school corridor, leaning in close for the kiss, his chest rubbing against her breasts, her hands on his ass, grinding his front into her. It was all he wanted for the night.

And then a sentence spoken to him earlier hit him hard. 'The past comes back to remind us that we haven't moved at all.'

"What happened?" Renee asked.

"Nothing. Absolutely nothing," he lied and looked out of the window as she continued to do her number on him.

Anay woke up in the middle of the night in his little apartment, gasping for breath. It was a warm summer night when he had gone to sleep, but now his room was unbearably cold. Still in half-sleep, he found his quilt and pulled it over himself. The night was still dark, and in the snugness of the quilt, his head fell easy on the pillow again, his eyes closed, and sleep began to engulf him.

These were the moments he hated.

Three years ago, when he had moved to the big city, alone, he did not realize what a lonely struggle it would be. He had been one of the fortunate ones to have found work and company right away, but he also knew that those weren't there to stay. He came from a large family, one where all his needs had been always taken care of, including preparing and serving his meals. Here, in the dingy apartments that he got to stay in, he had to wash his own plates and underwear. There was the time when he fell ill for a week. That was when he was compelled to call back home, knowing that just a soothing word from someone he had grown up with might make him better. But he stopped short of pressing the green button on the phone. He could not make the call. Wouldn't it be selfish calling home only when you needed them?

There was the noise again, the noise that had woken him up. A flapping noise. Not unlike the wings of a bird.

Fucking hallucinations! Those came with the loneliness, he guessed. He had lost count of the number of nights when he had been aroused in the middle of the sleep like this and opened his eyes to a dark, empty apartment. That feeling that something had been sitting on his chest and was still there now watching him from some corner of the room, was unshakeable. Whenever that feeling came over, it undid everything that he had done. He forgot all his joys, all his successes, and only remembered that he was terribly, terribly alone, and the ghosts of his loneliness were looking back at him.

It happened again. This time, much more furious. Like it was right there in front of him.

All at once, he knew with a rising dread that this night was different. Had some night bird entered the house?

He opened his eyes. With great discomfort, he blinked several times to acclimatize to the darkness. For a moment, he saw nothing.

And then, he almost died at the sight in front of him.

Dangling from a corner of the ceiling, covering an entire one-fourth of it, was a large black mass. He could not tell at once what it was; it looked like an infestation of mold on the walls. But there was the constant sound of movement, like something fluttering in the breeze. And he saw the sides of it moving, like many waves on the ocean. And then, his terror-filled eyes fell on the prime spot of this billowing blight.

It was a rounder area with a prominent protuberance. He could tell nothing of it though... and then, with the swiftness of a memory attacking the mind, he realized it was a head.

He was sure when the eyes opened. Blue blazing orbs, piercing their way to him in the darkness.

He did not know if he passed out then or fell asleep, for the blackness that surrounded him until morning was absolute.

Chapter 3

There was something odd in the air around him; Anay could not deny that. Apart from the nightmares and the visions, he could feel its material presence. At times it was as subtle as a shadowy mist trying to manifest out of thin air, while at other times it was as overwhelming as the incessant buzzing of a bee. Often, especially when alone, he could feel that sudden chill passing through the entirety of his body, making him shiver with a jerk. He could sense it around him, but whenever he turned to look, he would be met with nothingness.

He put it down to a stressful time at work—the only logical explanation he could see. The cat-food project had been bagged, but the client turned out to be, as his boss put it, 'a finicky bastard.' "It is usually the case with people who pay promptly," Salil told him. "They pay quickly so that they can control the strings. Remember this life-lesson, kid!" Anay knew that life-lesson already, and to make it worth the investment that Sen had made for his cat-food marketing, Anay burned the midnight lamp. Right from closing the script for the final version of the ad to auditioning the cats, he was hands-on. He also knew that Salil was watching every step; he was under a microscope and what he showed of himself under that magnification could make or break his career in the industry.

Anay's upbringing had been in an interior town in central India. Indore could hardly be called as a small town, but it definitely wasn't Mumbai. At his school in Indorethe Holy Heart Conventhe had shone through. But the admiration of his accolades in school did not extend to his home. He was the middle of three brothers, which led to an inevitable lack of parental attention. When the third brother was born, his father, Gopal Chandra Ghosh, decided that he had enough heirs to run his huge textile business. That was what had been drummed into the boys' heads from their youngest days, which was why things like academic marks and grades did not matter.

But Anay was different. He did not want what his family offered him. He had dreams of a big city life. Even as a child, he would run behind express trains on the open tracks, imagining that he was going to either Mumbai or Bangalore or Delhi, the big cities that he had heard of, especially Mumbai because that was where the business of glamor was, where he could rub shoulders with the movie stars.

When his father passed away suddenly soon after his schooling years, he saw his dream taking a more concrete shape. He focused on making a life one day in the big city. He studied hard and the degrees followed. Soon after his graduation in media marketing, he made the bold move of applying for a job in Mumbai. It was the catharsis to his childhood ailment of being stuck in a town that wasn't a metropolis.

But it came at a costhis older brother threatened to obliterate him from the flourishing family business. Anay could not care less.

Now, at an annual package of fifteen lakh rupees which was slated to increase soon, he was one of the most contented men of his age in Mumbai. Still in his twenties, he had the world to conquer.

But good things have a way of not lasting forever. Their ultimate cruelty lies in the fact that they create an illusion of permanence, which makes it all the more difficult when they sneak away without a goodbye.

Somewhere around him, Anay could feel that cloud too; a mist of despair that something was amiss, that this veneer of happiness would dissipate soon and he would be left behind with nothing but the bare bones of his loneliness, and it was this insecurity that besmirched his joys of satisfaction.

A few days after that night at The Bandana, a curious incident happened that boosted this notion in his mind.

It was mid-morning, around eleven. Anay had stepped out for the dubbing studio, which was a half-hour's ride from the office of Changemakers. His task was to check the final cut of the cat-food ad. It was early morning yet according to media industry timings. When he reached the studio, an assistant was still cleaning up the place. Looking at Anay, the thin reedy boy in a shirt with open buttons and jeans folded up to his knees, went into a tizzy. He profusely apologized for having forgotten the appointment and led Anay right away into the dubbing room.

"Sorry, sir," he said. "Everything is ready. Just a minute and I'll hook it up. Our sound recordist will be arriving shortly. If you want, you can watch the ad until then."

Anay took up on the offer. In fact, he was thankful for the opportunity to watch the ad alone in the dubbing studio. He followed the assistant into the small twelve-feet-by-twelve-feet viewing room. The dubbing area was beyond it, separated by a glass partition and a dark curtain. Anay, with his height of six feet one inch, had to stoop in the studio. He quickly slumped on the chair in front of the large-screen computer and waited for it to boot up.

The assistant left after opening the file on the computer. Anay rolled up his sleeves and relaxed. The lights in the room were all off, and save for the light from the computer screen, there was no other illumination. Rubbing his hands together, which was something he did when excited, he hit on the play button.

He had watched the ad dozens of times before. In fact, he knew each and everything about it—each syllable of dialog, each inch of location, each shred of costume, everything. He had been there since its conception, of course; nothing had passed to screen without his knowledge.

And, of course, he knew the cats.

There were three of them—a brown spotted tabby, a white Chinese cat, and a black Burmese cat. In the ad, they were in their respective homes, their humans fawning over them and petting them. The ad began with the cats being sad and lonely despite everything their families did for them, which was when they decided to purchase the new product in town, and, voilà! The cats were resurrected from sheer misery and transformed into studs around town. In a final scene, the felines walked along the streets of the city like cowboys, purring with contentment at being fed their favorite cereal.

Anay laughed at the last scene, which was the source of the humor.

He watched it thrice, and it was then—at the end of the third viewing—that he felt he saw something after the last freeze shot.

He played it again.

It was when the three cats were gallivanting on the streets. The black cat, whose name was Harrie (with an 'ie' and not a 'y' as his owner had expressly stated at the first meeting), was the object of his attention. The bizarre thing was, even after the ad ended and the frame froze, the black cat appeared to move.

It was the most bizarre thing. Harrie appeared to raise his paw and look at something in the distance. With that, the cat's face turned to a terrified expression with his large eyes bulging out and staring, his pupils reduced to mere pinpricks. But it was horrifying, for all of this happened after everything on screen had come to a complete standstill.

It was unbelievable! Anay lost a beat the first time he saw it. He remembered someone telling him about the psychic sense of cats. But these cats were not even real right now; they were on screen. That made everything all the more terrifying.

"Fuck! What's this?" Anay said aloud and played it for the tenth time. It appeared as if the cat was looking at something behind Anay, trying to show him whatever it was. Anay turned back to look. But that was a foolish notion, of course! The dubbing room was so small that if he pushed his chair behind, he would touch the sound-proofed wall behind him. "It's a weird glitch," he noted as the same movement repeated a dozen times.

But the moment he said that, there was a soft but terribly frightening meow, which echoed in the room just after the ad jingle stopped.

Anay sprang up in sheer fright, his head hitting the ceiling. The meow had happened on screen for sure, but with it there was something moving in the dubbing area beyond the glass partition, which was in utter darkness. Anay felt something growing within his chest now, a knot of fear. And this only increased when he looked in the direction of the dubbing area.

There was something moving in there, in the darkness.

He rushed out of the dubbing room, sweating and breathing hard. He headed right up to the water dispenser and emptied an entire glass and splashed another on his face. He sat down on the sofa in the outer area, which was brightly lit and had a ceiling fan rotating at full speed. Leaning as far back as he could, he tried to gather his breath.

"What's it, sir?" said the assistant, coming out of the pantry. "Is it hot inside?"

Anay's shirt was drenched with both perspiration and the water he had splashed upon himself. He tried to say something but realized that he would only come out looking foolish in front of this stranger. Instead he said, "Nothing. Just trying to catch my breath."

"Sure! Here's your coffee," said the assistant.

Anay took a cup from the tray. "Thanks. Needed that."

And then, he was gripped by another surge of fear. He saw the assistant walking into the dubbing room. There was another cup of coffee on the tray.

"Wh-who is that coffee for?" Anay asked him.

"Well, sir, for your friend who was sitting inside with you."

Anay almost died.

CHAPTER 4

Anay was in his cabin pulling his hair out. He could dismiss his nocturnal visions as his overworked and lonely mind imagining things, but what about this invisible stalker that people were talking about? Invisible to him, for others appeared to see him. That was the most frustrating thing about it.

The studio assistant could not describe him well. "Only saw him for a moment in the studio with you. Didn't see him properly because of all the darkness. But he had his hand on your shoulder, so I thought he was your friend. Why, sir? Is there any problem?"

"No, nothing's wrong," Anay said. Such a kind of thing is not worth getting deep into, he told himself. He is surely making a mistake like everyone else. He sees dozens of people in the studio every day and is just confused. What else can it be?

Unless, the whole universe was somehow playing a grand prank on him.

An hour later, he somehow managed to get back to his work, trying to keep his mind cool. But his mind wasn't what it used to be. It wasn't just the scary things that were happening. It was also the lack of sleep, the frustration of meeting the deadlines, and that tiny niggling bug that had lately being gnawing at him Was it worth breaking his neck so much over work?

He jumped with a start when his phone rang. When he saw who it was, he took the call instantly.

"Oh, hi, Shanaya," he said, altering his tone to a cheerier one to whatever extent it was possible. "To what do I owe this pleasure?"

Shanaya laughed. Even her muffled laughter from the other end of the phone line sounded like a lilting melody. "Hi, Anay. Wondering if I could meet you today."

"Wow, of course! I mean, of course... what do you... I mean, when do you want to meet?"

"Say in an hour in that coffee shop across the street from your office? I am in the area, doing some shopping. Thought I'd drop in and check on you."

"All right, done. I'll be there."

"You can get away from your office, no? It won't be a problem, right?"

"No problem at all!"

She laughed again and disconnected the phone.

Anay quickly surveyed himself in the office mirror. He looked good, apart from the dark circles under his eyes. He should have shaved that morning, or did the stubble suit him better? He was better with the stubble. He had time to shave, but he ran the risk of looking like a junior college student. Should he get her a gift? Of course not. This was not a date. She was just dropping in. But she was his childhood flame!

He checked in on Kautuk. "Hey, buddy! Just stepping out for an hour. You will be able to manage if Salil asks about me?"

"I'll try," Kautuk muttered, not looking up from his browser, and expertly throwing a peanut in his mouth. "Work or pleasure, may I ask?"

"No, you may not!" Anay laughed and retreated.

Briskly, he stepped into the elevator. It was in the foyer that he bumped into the familiar—in fact, too familiar—deodorant of Renee.

"Where to?" Renee asked.

"Just stepping out for a bit."

"Wait, wait. This is not for a regular meeting."

"I'm getting late, Renee."

Renee sized him up. "Are you up to something, Anay?"

Just then, Anay spotted Vishwa walking toward the elevators. He had never been happier to see him. "Hey, look! There's Vishwa," he screamed.

Vishwa noticed and began walking up to them.

"I don't like this, Anay," Renee whispered. "Something's going on here."

Vishwa caught up. "What's the matter, dude?"

Anay thought quickly. "Hey, not much. Just going out for a meeting. Just keep a lookout if Salil notices my absence."

Without waiting for a reply or turning back at Renee, he stepped out of the automatic office doors.

Shanaya was dressed in typical casual office-wear—a red loose top paired with blue denims—but he still could not take his eyes off her. She had evidently made no effort to look pretty for him, because her hair was unbrushed and tied in a high bun, leaving some strands dangling down over her ears. She was wearing simple earrings, small hoops of gold that complimented her slender neck. He was glad that she had not worked on her appearance before he arrived; that took a lot of pressure off his shoulders. And there was also that little fact—she was the one who had called him. Why should he feel the butterflies in his belly then? He asked his thumping heart to stay still.

"How was the week?" Shanaya asked.

He knew she didn't really want the answer to that question. He kept it as short as he could. "It was okay."

They chatted for a while and coffees were ordered. They chatted more till they arrived, and then Shanaya cleared her throat. "Listen, Anay, so the thing is... I am not happy with where I am working. It's not challenging work. All I have to do is to keep records of the jewelry they sell every day. It's a sitting job staring at a computer screen. I want to move on."

"Yes, yes, of course you should," Anay said in the tone of a great guru dispensing life advice.

"I want to do something creative. Something like you do. I am ready to work my way upward."

Anay's heart missed a beat. She liked what he did!

"So, I am asking," she went on, "is there a position at Changemakers? Even the most junior position will do."

"I'll see what I can do," Anay said heartily. "I am sure there will be a spot for you."

It was then that he saw that her lipstick was fresh. It was still glittering like it had been applied recently, just moments before he arrived. There was probably a purpose to this meeting, after all.

"I will be so grateful," Shanaya said. "I just want to get out of the clutches of my sleazy boss. I don't want to talk any more about it, but I hope you understand."

He did. In fact, he was already dreaming about her in the same office space as him. They would be able to bump into each other all the time. Over time, he'd ask her to join his core team, and maybe take her to the client meetings. Maybe even some of those outstation ones. Eventually sharing a hotel room. He shook himself back to reality. Building castles in the air never did work well for anyone.

"I'll check," he said, checking his eagerness. "I will ask Salil, my boss."

"Oh, that would be great!"

"We are actually short-staffed and with the new mega project we have just landed. I think it will be easy to convince Salil about a new hand. I could easily talk to our HR" He stopped there abruptly, not knowing why he did that. The HR head was Renee. She would definitely ask a million questions.

"I will be thankful," she said. "Now let me treat you to some early lunch."

Anay did not refuse that offer. They did not talk any more about work, but chatted their way through a meal of pizzas, trying to fill in the gaps between what they had been doing in the intervening years from school to now. Anay hardly ate while she did all the talking. There were times during the conversation when he did not even listen to her. He just kept staring into her eyes and her lips as she spoke with great fascination of the times gone by, their many teachers and friends, and punctuated every sentence with short laughs, showing her perfect set of teeth. It fascinated him how little everything had changed. He was still that same schoolboy smitten by the prettiest girl in class.

"Let me grab the check," she said abruptly, and he came back to his senses. "I insist. I called you; it's only fair."

He watched her go to the counter. Her gait was brisk and casual, not the hyper-accentuated sashaying catwalk he had seen on so many wannabe girls. She had evolved into the full package indeed, the woman who always had a purpose.

Anay looked ahead, out of the window of the café. This is a good thing, he told himself. She is the right one for you, and you for her. Don't fuck this up.

But then, as it was happening with him lately, he saw behind that pretty smile of hers and beyond those alluring eyes. Like something wrenching his heart, he felt a severe pang that this was not going to happen, whatever he was thinking about. That negative aura that he had been sensing of late was soon going to make its appearance.

And then it did.

There was something in the corner of the café. He could feel the terrifying vibe. There was a movement. Up somewhere, in the walls. The nasty feeling of dread filled him. A current ran from his neck to his fingers. Why now? Why did he have to feel this now when everything was going so well? When he was with her, the woman of his dreams? Like drops of water on a red-hot pan, his amorous thoughts sizzled away and vanished.

He looked around. The café was full of people, carrying on with their routine everyday talk. Unsuspecting people. But he shook away his jumpiness. What can happen in such a place?he tried to justify to himself.

Shanaya was at the counter making the payment, laughing about something the man behind the counter had told her as he handed her card back to her. She took it and returned to Anay. Anay stood up and joined her. He held her arm instinctively then, but quickly pulled back. What if she did not like it? All the same, he wanted to touch her again. Oh, damn! That softness of her arm! In that moment, he forgot what he had just sensed. There was nothing in the world that he wanted to touch so bad.

They turned to move toward the door, and it was at that precise moment that there was a loud crash.

Anay spun around to look. The sight was beyond his wildest imaginations.

A portion of the ceiling had caved in.

Chapter 5

All at once, daylight exploded into the mood-lit interiors of the café. A large cloud of dust had risen, the particles still flying all around. Pieces of rubble had flown in every direction, smashing objects, hitting the walls, even falling on people. And then someone screamed. Anay looked at her. She was a girl, holding her forehead, stemming blood from the fresh wound. Someone else looked dazed at his laptop, whose screen was smashed by another fragment of the rubble. The very next moment, collective screams of people rent the place. Someone stood up and rushed to the door, and then another followed. What had been a normal day at the café turned to a scene of pandemonium within seconds, as everyone rose at once to get to the nearest way out of the café.

Anay stood rooted to the spot in utter shock. He had realized that the debris had fallen on the exact spot where Shanaya had been standing making the payment moments ago.

"Shanaya! Shanaya!" he screamed, looking at the mound of rubble now on the floor next to the payment counter.

There was no reply.

Something inside him blacked out. He lost all hope in that moment. Something just snapped. He knew he would not get past this. This was not meant to happen. He had just met Shanaya; hadn't even got to know her well. Was she there? Trapped under the debris? Tears and shock took hold of him.

Another portion of the ceiling collapsed, this time right behind him. The glass façade crashed. People screamed again, those stragglers who hadn't yet been able to find their way out. Anay saw, with great horror, that a splinter was embedded in his arm. A tiny one, but it brought him back to his senses.

Then he heard a shout, "HEY, YOU! HELP ME OUTTA HERE!" It was the man behind the counter, apparently the owner, who had just been laughing with Shanaya.

"Shanaya! Where is Shanaya?" Anay asked.

He came running to the mound and began to look. No, it didn't seem that she was under that slab. No, of course not! She wasn't there! She must have run out! Joy suddenly swept over him as that thought struck him.

"Hey, help me!" the man screamed again.

This time, Anay looked at him closely and then stared, wide-eyed. The man was trapped. Part of the roof had fallen directly over the counter. Anay leaned over the counter and saw the man's leg was trapped under the rubble.

Anay looked around. The café was almost empty now; Shanaya had definitely run out. Outside, there was chaos. But this man was in here. He could not leave him. He hopped over the counter and said, "I'll get you out, man!" Furiously, he began removing the pieces of debris around the man's leg.

"That hurts!" the man screamed as Anay tried to shift a particular piece of concrete that was right over his knee, which was evidently broken.

"Hang on!" said Anay. "This is heavy, but I'll get help." But as he said that, there was another rumbling. Anay looked up in fear. Another portion of the roof's concrete was now dangling precariously right above their heads, and this was a much larger piece. It had parted away from the beam structure on three sides and was now just dangling from a fourth. It could fall down at any moment.

"There's no time!" Anay screamed. "Try to move, man!"

The man winced as he put all his strength into moving his foot, ignoring all the pain. He lashed around his arms to try to move, but the slab of debris on him was too heavy. And then, it moved. If only by a fraction, it moved.

The man screamed, "Try to take it off now! Do it now!"

Anay bent to do whatever he could. He put his hands on the slab, not caring that its jagged ends now punctured his own flesh and grunted as hard as he could.

Overhead, there was another rumble.

Anay did not let go of the slab. It was somewhat loosened now. A few more heaves and it would be out of the way. But was there time?

Then Anay made the mistake of looking up again. He looked at the broken ceiling. Out of the gaping hole, where the sky was exposed, Anay saw it

that same ghastly thing writhing along its edges. That dark entity that he had seen in his room, with its blue blazing eyes and billowing arms. It was there, wrenched in that gap on the roof. It was trying to bring the rest of that slab down.

"Go away!" Anay yelled. "Go away. Don't do this!"

"Motherfucker! What are you doing?" the trapped man screamed. "Move the slab!"

Anay juddered and fell backward. The creature or whatever it was had brought down the ceiling. Its arms were now moving forth, moving toward Anay as if to stop him. Anay froze. The thing glided and placed its mouth on the man's neck.

"No..." Anay yelled. "Don't do it. Let me save him."

The words just rushed out of Anay's mouth in a pleading voice that he had never heard on himself before.

But a part of him knew that he could not save the man. He was doomed. He could hear the man's cries and abuses and shouts, but there was nothing to be done. The man was in the grip of that agent of death. Something pushed Anay back, a cold piercing force that he could not explain, and he was thrown off toward the door of the café. He was still crawling on the floor, when that remaining portion of the slab gave way and collapsed right on the skull of the poor man.

His final scream was cut off midway as the slab shattered his jawbone right into his vocal cords.

The sirens of various emergency vehicles filled the atmosphere. The stunned Anay was shoved by someone to the other side of the road, away from the crash site. He was still shaking, having lost all control and consciousness, not knowing what strange hell he had been pushed into, when he saw him again─the perpetrator of all this doom.

The entity stood there in the middle of the ruined café, unaffected by the falling debris and the clouds of dust everywhere around, and unperturbed by the crowds running helter-skelter. Though Anay could not see the facial features, he could sense that there was a smile lurking in those cold blue lips. And he could tell it was a sneer of malevolence.

Anay took a while to spot Shanaya. In the mayhem that had ensued, she had run ahead, pushed on by the screaming people.

"Oh my God, Anay! You are all bloody. Are you fine? Are you all right?" she said without a pause.

"I am fine," he said, his voice phlegmy because of the nausea. He could say nothing more.

"What happened there, Anay? Why did you take so long to come out?"

"That guy," said Anay, his voice and body both trembling. "He was trapped. I tried to get him out... but..."

"Oh damn, what happened to him?"

Anay felt something behind him. Immediately thinking of the shadowy figure, and scared to bits, he turned to look. It was just a mother dragging her child away from the scene.

He stole a look at the café, terrified as to what he might see there, and noticed that a police van had reached the spot. An inspector was surveying the area. He was asking zapped bystanders a few questions. One of the bystanders pointed at him. The inspector looked at him, and the next moment, he was by their side.

"You were the last to come out of the café?" the inspector asked gruffly.

"Y-yes..." Anay mumbled.

"Where were you sitting?"

"Near... near the counter."

"What exactly happened?"

Shanaya answered this one. "We just settled our check when there was a rumbling sound. A small portion of the roof fell first and everyone started to run out. I ran out too, thinking that Anay was following me."

"Was he with you?"

"No... I thought... I thought Shanaya was trapped under the debris."

"Do you know the man who died?"

"I was trying to help him..." Anay mumbled.

"But he is dead," the policeman said.

"I... I couldn't get him out."

The inspector gave him a nasty look. "Why not? Did you even try?"

Anay turned to Shanaya, shocked. "Is it my mistake that man is dead?"

"Of course not!" Shanaya said firmly. "Sir, my friend was in shock. He could not even move. How could he have saved that man when he himself was paralyzed with fear?"

The inspector shook his head and walked away. He said something to his constable and they both laughed derisively.

"You are badly shaken," Shanaya told Anay, drawing his attention away from the insensitive policeman. "I understand the state you were in. Here, hold my hand. Where do you want to go now?"

"To the office... office..."

"Come on; it's right across the street. Let me take you."

His head was buzzing. His eardrums reverberated with a tinny sound. The spots in front of his eyes would not stop. He allowed her to grab his arm. There was already a traffic chaos on the street. None of the vehicles were able to move. Two fire-brigade engines had arrived, but they weren't able to maneuver the street and navigate into the smaller alley where the café was. Had been. Shanaya led him by the arm. They crossed the road together, finding their way through the stalled vehicles incessantly blaring their horns. On the other side of the street, they came to the tall glass-walled office building. She got Anay into the elevator. On the eleventh floor, it stopped and she helped Anay out.

The security guard came running up to them. He was horrified to see Anay's condition—his tattered clothes, his disarrayed hair, his shaking body. "What happened?" he asked.

"We were in the café opposite."

"Oh, no!" the security-man said. Evidently the news of the collapse had reached the office. It would be in the news all over the city shortly. Without any further question, the guard brought them into the lobby and made them sit in the waiting area. The receptionist at the welcoming desk let out a shriek and ran inside to call someone.

Renee, Vishwa, and Kautuk came rushing out at once. While Kautuk took the chair next to Anay and propped him up on his arm, and Vishwa ran to grab a bottle of water, Renee checked for any wounds. Shanaya stepped back as the friends took over.

"I hope you are not hurt, Anay..." Renee said. "We heard about the crash. Heard the owner died. Fuck, are you all right?"

Anay nodded.

"Glad to know you still have your life, bro!" Kautuk patted his back. "Everything else will heal."

Vishwa came back. "Should we take you to the hospital? There might be some hidden injuries, man..."

"I'm all right," Anay said. "Just a bit shaken, that's all."

Renee spotted Shanaya. "Hi. You were with him?"

"She's Shanaya," Anay replied. "My schooltime buddy."

"Oh!" Renee's look said more than it expressed. "Thanks for bringing him here."

"I must leave now," said Shanaya. "Anay, see you later, okay?"

Anay nodded. He raised his head to look at her with some difficulty and gave her a warm goodbye smile.

Kautuk chimed in, "You two go ahead. I'll sit with him for a while."

"Are you sure?" Vishwa asked.

"Go on, man."

Vishwa and Renee patted Anay on his arm and spoke a few things softly to him and then ducked inside. Kautuk did not move from his seat, nor did he take away the arm on which Anay was resting his head. After a few minutes, he asked, "What do you want to do?"

"Take me home, man! I just need to lie down."

Kautuk ducked in and brought out both their bags, and then signaled to the receptionist that they were signing out for the day.

Chapter 6

"So now I have told you everything… what do you think?"

Anay was sitting on the bed of his apartment, while Kautuk was in a chair across him. He had brought Anay to the house, done some first aid on the wound on his arm, and prepared some coffee. Over coffee, Anay recounted to him about all the bizarre things that had gripped his life of late.

"You mean to say there's someone following you? Other people can see him, but you cannot?" Kautuk said.

"It has been happening for a while," Anay said, nodding to himself. "Ever since I moved to Mumbai, in fact. At first, I could not see it, but people around me could. Like, there was this one time I went to a restaurant for dinner. I was alone. But when the waiter came, he brought two glasses of water. I did not think much about it, thinking it was their standard practice. But then, when I was placing the order, the waiter asked me if my friend was coming back and if I wanted to order for him too. When I said I had come alone, he gave me and odd look and went his way. I did not think much about it. Then, when I came to Changemakers on my first interview, I entered the elevator alone.

There was an old man operating the elevator. He asked me which floor I wanted to go. I said eleventh. He pressed the button for my floor, and then looked beside me and asked, 'And you, sir?' There was no reply. The man then shook his head and said, 'That's funny! I could have sworn someone entered the elevator with you.' That was the first time I was shocked. I didn't know what to say."

"Weird. What did you think about it?"

"That they were coincidences. What else could they be? But these days, especially since last week, I am feeling it too. I am actually seeing things, Kautuk. I saw it the first time at Bandana on the night I met Shanaya. Then I saw it in the dubbing studio and at the café. It was threatening me, smiling at me. Oh God, I cannot think of that creature now. It's the scariest thing I have seen. I know it's out to get me."

"Creature? Is your stalker a man or a creature?"

"I don't know. People tell me he's a man, but I have seen him as a frightful creature. It was he who caused the collapse at the café, but who can I tell that to?"

Kautuk pondered over that. "What did the waiter and the elevator guy say? You must have asked them to describe the guy they saw with you."

"At first, I didn't ask. It was too ridiculous. But then I did. The description is more or less the same—a medium-sized guy with curly hair and glasses. That's who they see with me. But I don't know anyone with that appearance."

"And the creature you see?"

"Oh, he's terrifying. See up there on the ceiling? I saw him right there the other night. Like a black tarry mass oozing out of the wall. He had a face, though. Horrible thing with blue eyes. I cannot forget those eyes."

Kautuk looked up at the ceiling and shivered. "Creepy stuff, for sure," he said, and then leaned forward. "See, brother, our mind plays many tricks on us. And, according to what you told me, your mental state was disturbed whenever you saw this thing, whatever it is. At the washroom at Bandana, you were extremely nervous about the deal earlier that day, and today the roof literally fell on your head. It is understandable that your inner fears are playing out."

"What fears do I have?"

"Could be anything. Some inner phobia, perhaps. Then there is the fact that you are in a new city which is different from your hometown. You just moved into this new house in this new locality. It happens to all of us. I live with my parents, but I feel lonely too. Barely any friends except you guys, you see? I see things sometimes too. You told me once when we were drunk about your loneliness, remember? You live alone in this apartment far removed from the main road. All you can see out of your house is the desolate part of the beach. In the dark when sleeping alone like this in small apartments, surrounded by absolute darkness, your mind must get fucked up, maybe just subconsciously. You are living this constant nightmare of loneliness. That's all it is."

"You think so?"

"I am absolutely sure it is so. You must not think too much about it either. Thoughts generate more thoughts of the same kind. They are cohesive, you know? Like how drops of water attract each other and form a larger drop? That's how our fears are. Our smaller fears aggregate over time and become a giant paranoia. You must step away before you are caught up in a web of your phobias."

"What do I do to not be alone in this house?"

"Now that I cannot answer," said Kautuk with a smile.

Anay took a long look at Kautuk and managed a lopsided grin. "You talk like some saint, buddy! What the fuck are you doing in an ad company?"

"Bringing some saintliness into the devil's world, that's what."

The friends laughed. Kautuk took away Anay's cup and kept it in the kitchen. It had turned dark. He switched on the lights of the house. He then shouted from the kitchen as if a new thought had struck him, "Dude, what is this deal with the new girl?"

"What do you mean by deal?" Anay shouted back.

Kautuk walked back in. "Well, she does make you smile a lot, doesn't she?"

Anay grinned. "Do you think so?"

"I have seen it. Don't forget that nothing escapes the attention of Kautuk Tiwari."

"Well, she was a crush."

"I thought she was just a school friend."

"It was more than that. At least, on my side."

"There it is!"

"I just bumped into her all of a sudden that night at Bandana," Anay said. "Not that I am complaining."

"Are you dating?"

"No, no. Just met twice. At Bandana and today at the café."

"Hmm..."

"What was that?"

Kautuk shook his head. "Just a funny thought, that's all."

"What?"

"You have any associated memories with her? Good ones? Bad ones?"

"Well, we kissed once back then."

"That's a good memory then."

"Yeah. What are you trying to say?"

"I will say no further because I value our friendship."

"If you value our friendship, you will say it."

Anay stood up now. He looked down at Kautuk, which made him look more forceful than his mental state warranted.

"Come on, it's probably nothing," Kautuk waved.

"Say it."

"Okay, then. I have read that all of us have an aura. An energy around us, so to speak. We don't see this energy, but we can feel it in other people. It sometimes also affects us. Don't we meet someone and our day suddenly becomes brighter and everything goes right? And sometimes don't we feel completely fucked up after meeting someone? It is because of the energy people radiate. Now I will say no more."

Kautuk picked up his bag. "Do you want me to stay the night? I could, if you want. I'll just crash on the couch or something."

"No, I am fine. Thanks, buddy," Anay said.

"Are you sure?"

"Yes, yes. You have done enough for today."

"Then I need to leave now to reach home before ten. Take care, then," Kautuk said, hoisting his bag on his shoulders.

After Kautuk left, Anay stood in the middle of the room, shaking. Energies? Auras? He had heard of them too. Everyone had it. But what had Kautuk been alluding to? It sounded like some superstitious crap. Just the kind of warped thing Kautuk would say. Nah, he did not believe in that kind of stuff. Kautuk was a raving fool.

Laughing aloud, he fell back on the bed.

CHAPTER 7

Hundreds of thoughts beleaguered Anay's mind all at once, but none of them seemed to make sense. It was a week after the ghastly incident at the café. As was expected, the news had hit the papers, with one report subtly referring to him in unflattering words:

Hemant Dahiya, the owner of The Brown Bun café, was the only casualty. Trapped under the debris of the first collapse, Dahiya, could not get himself out in time and bore the brunt of the fatal second collapse. He might have had a shot at survival if the last customer to leave the collapsing café, an able-bodied gentleman working at a nearby office, had managed to pull him out. Despite seeing Dahiya trapped under the rubble, the young man rushed out of the café without attempting to help. It is a stark reflection of the times we are living in that we cannot pause a moment to save someone even from a mortal peril.

Never cried in ages, that day Anay felt the tears flow down his cheeks. There it was, in black and white how he had not rescued a man from his death, which, as the report seemed to suggest, was tantamount to murdering him. He rationalized it to himself that it was not true, and that was what Shanaya told him repeatedly on the phone as well, but he could not bear to stay unaffected by that guilt. It was a café he had visited often. He had seen that man on countless occasions, and probably even spoken to him at some point, and now his blood was on his hands.

That night, Hemant Dahiya was the subject of his nightmares. In the middle of the night, he saw the face of the man, at first smiling, and then rapidly convulsed with fear as he yelled, "Help me out of here!" The next instant, the face was smashed beyond recognition, and from that distorted mouth came accusatory words:

"You could have saved me but you didn't."

Anay woke up sweating and gasping. He could not stay in that bedroom; it was beginning to choke him. Kautuk was right about the loneliness. He went to the balcony and stood there smoking, gazing at the languorous waves of the sea in the distance. It was three-thirty in the morning. He had no courage to go back to that empty and dark bedroom. At least here in the balcony, he could see the outside world even though there was not a soul on the streets. It lent him a measure of comfort.

His mind raced to the things that were tormenting him. There was only thing he could think of the invisible man who was stalking him. He shut his eyes and tried all he could to visualize the man. Had he seen anyone like that? Curly hair? Glasses? It wasn't a very unique description. Of course, on the streets out there, there were thousands of such men. But, try as he might, he could not think of ever having interacting with any such man in person.

There was another angle that he could pursue. Why could be the motive of such a thing? Perhaps it was all a huge conspiracy. That was his first thought. Maybe they were all in it the lift-operator, the waiter, the dubbing studio assistant, even the peon Sudhir. They were all in cahoots and playing some trick on him. That seemed to be the only logical explanation. But why would anyone go to that extent? Was he such an important person that someone might hatch such a plot against him?

It was his fault too. He had not been active in his investigation yet. He didn't go back to the dubbing studio to check if there was someone else. Or check the camera in the conference room that day. Perhaps, he didn't have the courage to check for some reason. But the answer could emerge if he just made a small effort. So, that was what he resolved to do. He was a fighter. The next time anyone told him there was an invisible man near him, he would grab them by the neck and ask them more questions.

The cigarette butt burned out in his hand and he threw it away with a jerk and immediately lit up another. The night was pleasant. The cool breeze from the sea was one of its biggest advantages, as Renee had said, and it was all out in its full glory right now. He felt the breeze on him, letting him wash away his worries at least for the moment. It was such a beautiful night that he scolded himself for thinking of the unsavory elements of his life.

He forced himself to think of something pleasant. And he immediately knew what it was. The moment he closed his eyes, Shanaya's face danced in front of him. Would it be appropriate to send her a message at this hour? It was nearing four a.m. What if, in the slightest off-chance, she was awake and might chat with him? He did not have the courage to do that either, for he knew he'd regret such a thing in the morning. He decided to satisfy himself with her thoughts, aware that she was the only thing that made him truly happy at the moment.

He carried one of the four plastic chairs he had in his apartment into the balcony and sat on it. Gazing at the stars and the waves outside, he channeled his thoughts to the girl of his dreams. Would she be his? His mind went back to the kiss of his boyhood. Every tactile impulse of that touch came alive to him again. He felt her on his lips. He felt her in his groin. It was just like his school nights, when he would be on the bed of the room of his parents' house and let go of himself, fantasizing about her in various ways. Nothing had changed! Slowly, his fear and worry began to transform into pleasure. Yes, that was what he liked. Not the thoughts of stalkers and ghosts.

He wanted to prolong the moment. Slumping down in one chair, he propped up his legs on another and let his hand stray into his shorts. Powering his phone on with his other hand, he scrolled down her messages. The messages were innocuous little things, exchanged over the past few days that they had been in touch, but they were enough to set his lonely desires on the edge. There were the everyday hellos and goodnights, and he read their subtext, especially the goodnights. What might she be doing when typing those goodnights? Lying down on her bed, surely. What might she be wearing? Of course, lying on her bed typing that goodnight, it was he she was thinking of. He enlarged her display picture and looked at her lips. A moan escaped his lips as he could not control himself anymore.

He threw his head back as the big moment arrived. He shut his eyes, now bringing every detail of her face and body to his mind, rapidly breathing and muttering things like, "Shan, if you will be mine, I'll do so much for you, my love!" It was such a profound thought, such an ardent desire, that he actually felt for a moment that she had spoken to him.

No, not in that imagined vision. For real. He really felt the soft breath brushing against his neck and something whispered in his ears.

All at once, he stopped and opened his eyes.

It was just for a flash, but he saw something before it vanished into the night.

It had been standing over him, astride on him as he lay on the chairs, looming in the air, its face staring down at him as he had been jacking off.

Shocked to bits, Anay fell out of the chairs and passed out. That was where he stayed for the rest of that night.

Chapter 8

The next morning, Anay had to rush to office. He had no time to think about the previous night. Salil had messaged a reminder to be on time for the meeting with Sen. He showered without soap and threw shirt and trousers on himself and got out of the house. On the way he thought about how he'd spend one more night alone in the apartment, but he pushed that thought for later. He had the difficult day to get through first.

The way it turned out; it wasn't a meeting to be proud of.

Everything had been done regarding the ad. Each input from Sen and his team had been incorporated. The creative team at Changemakers had been making sure the entire week to ensure that nothing that Sen wanted was left out. Salil did not want the balance payment to be pushed on to the next month. His express instruction to "close the fucking thing" had only served to put extra pressure on everyone.

Sen wasn't pleased. At least, not entirely. He reiterated the point he had been making since Day One. "I want something that will blow people's socks away. Something that will make them stop going to the loo during the ad break and sit up and take notice." And now he just sat there shaking his head. "It has not turned out the way I was promised," he said, looking directly at Anay across the table where the entire creative team was in attendance.

"Give us another week, sir," Anay said quickly. "One more week and we'll bring you the ad exactly as you see it."

"A week it is then," said Sen, standing up. "But only a week. I want the ad up before the product gets outdated. Just like human foods have fads, cat foods do too."

When Sen left, Anay crashed into his chair, deep in thought. Salil said, "Is there anything bothering you, Anay?"

"Not at all, sir," Anay said too quickly.

"Look at me, boy. You are here to work and make a name for yourself. A lot of eyes are on you. Everything depends on what steps you take here. You have a wonderful break at Changemakers, and I love you, but I can do only so much. The list of eager young men looking for similar breaks is too long, as you know."

With that not so veiled threat, Salil left the room. That was when Anay broke down and cursed the terrible turn his life was taking.

The only good thing about the day was that Shanaya called in the evening after leaving office. Anay quickly mended his disposition and they hopped over to The Bandana for dinner.

"Did you get a chance to talk to your boss?" she asked when they were done with their first round of beers.

"About?"

"About the job, Anay..."

"Oh, I will soon," he said and peered into his glass.

"My sleazy boss has started asking me to stay back at the office after everyone leaves. I have been making one excuse or the other so far. But one of these days..."

"He's an asshole," said Anay, flaring up. "Why don't you change your job and find something else?"

"I am looking, Anay. Apart from asking you, I have applied to a few other places too. But, you know, it will be special pleasure to work alongside you."

"I have no doubt of that." Anay attempted to smile. "I shall look forward to that day. We are currently busy with a difficult assignment. It has become a thorn in our side. My initial thought was to rope you in on this project, but it's not a good idea. Once I do this well, I shall have some negotiating power with my boss and get you in for sure."

There was silence for a while. Then she said, "I don't want you to think I am pestering you, okay? Please don't think I am meeting you only for a job."

"I know."

"I enjoy talking with you," Shanaya said. "Being with you is like being back home. All those school days..."

That thought made him genuinely smile. The carefree days of school! When nothing mattered; when he was king. There were no terrible ads to make, curbing one's own creativity and pandering to someone else's. It was so easy to impress doting teachers and fawning friends. Not like now when you had to kiss the ass of anyone who had money and called the shots.

"Those were fun days!" he said.

"Weren't they?" repeated Shanaya, excited. "I still remember so many things, like they happened just yesterday. All those friends we had... wonder what they are doing now. Do you remember them?"

"I don't think I do." Anay shrugged. "I am terrible with names and faces."

Shanaya laughed. "You would be!"

Anay laughed too. "What does that mean?"

"Why would you need to remember? You were the most desirable stud in school! Son of rich parents, strikingly handsome, and at the top of his game in everything."

"Really?"

"Compliment-fisher! Of course, ya! All the girls were crazy about you. I am sure some of the boys had a thing for you too!" She winked.

"Whoo, whoo, slow down! All the girls?"

Shanaya blushed.

"Not you?"

"Well, I won't say no. But we were such kids back then!"

Anay stared into her eyes with a mischievous smile dancing on his lips. "So, as long as we are confessing, let me tell you this. I had a major crush on you too."

"Really?"

"Of course! The boys could not stop chattering about you. They got haircuts to impress you! And when they talked about you, I used to feel like socking a punch in their bloody jaws. I felt for you so bad!"

There was more laughter.

"Do you remember the kiss?" she said.

A knot arose in Anay's throat. "Our first kiss..."

"Two young people, mad for each other, ended up sharing their first kiss," she said, "and then we were so embarrassed we hardly talked."

"I want to thank you, Shan," Anay said suddenly, his eyes turning a bit misty.

"What for?"

"I don't know if you feel it too, but this place has something about it," said Anay. "I used to think that a big city is all fun and glamor, and that is what we are all chasing, really, but at the end of the day, we are just lonely as hell. We are just feeding on this soulless city, like maggots feeding on a corpse."

"Oh, what an analogy! What brings that on, Anay?"

"The thing I want to tell you is... thanks for coming back into my life like this. I am not lonely here anymore. You know, when I left my family, it wasn't in the best of circumstances. For a while, I didn't think any of that mattered—family, friends. I still don't think, to be honest. But when you came here, it was like a breath of fresh air. I found a friend."

"Now don't get all sentimental on me, Anay!" Shanaya laughed. "You are a strong, motivated guy. You mustn't think about all these things."

"Nah, all of that... that attitude, that personality, is just on the surface. Beneath it all, I am just as lonely as any other bloke."

"Damn it! Let's have one more beer for you!" Shanaya snapped her fingers at a passing waiter and indicated an order for another pint. Then she said, "And as far as being lonely is concerned, you don't need to worry about it. I am here now."

It was the way she said it that did something to Anay. No, it was no commitment, but it was the exact thing he wanted to hear in that moment. He slid his hand across the table and felt her fingers tentatively. "Shan, tell me one thing," he said, moving up his hand on hers, carefully measuring her reaction. "Do you feel for me? I mean, do you think about me when I am not with you?"

"As a friend, ya!" she said with widened eyes, emphasizing the 'ya!'

"I mean more than that..." Anay said. "Last night, I was feeling so lonely, and all I could think of was you. I just wanted to message you, call you, and... and I hoped you were with me in my room."

She looked away, mumbling something incoherent. For a moment, Anay worried that he had angered her, but probably she was just bemused. There was no anger on her face.

He felt bold enough to ask her the question. "Shanaya..."

"What?"

"Look, don't get angry..."

"I won't. Why should I?"

"Look, I am always thinking about you. All the time. What if... I mean... would you come with me to my house tonight?"

There was a long moment of silence. She put her spoon and fork back into her plate and drank up her beer.

Anay's eyes did not leave her for a second. While deep in thought thus, she looked so much more desirable.

She narrowed her eyes, and he could not sit straight anymore. "Anay," she said, and there itself he knew what was coming. "It won't be appropriate, not at this time."

"Okay, sure. Of course, of course... I understand." In that moment, he wanted to kill himself. She had meant friend and he had taken it too far. He had screwed up the one good thing that he had going. Would she ever meet him again?

"Know this—you are the sexiest man I have ever met in person," she said. "But you see... we are both working here and something like that happens between us and doesn't work out, it will destroy both of us. I hope you understand."

Anay stammered with his words.

She took her hand away. Changing her tone, she said, "And with that, let's drop the subject. Shall we have some dessert?"

They had no dessert. For once, Anay could not wait to pay the check and get out of the accursed place where his humiliation had been put up on such prominent display.

Chapter 9

Bidding Shanaya goodbye at the pub itself, Anay walked out alone. He stepped out, unable to bear the uncomfortable silence any longer that had suddenly crept up between them.

He was hailing a cab when someone called out to him. He recognized the voice at once. He turned.

"Renee?"

She was dressed in a bold black gown, unbothered by all the male eyes around her that were trying to rest upon her. It appeared as if the gown was a deliberate attempt to remind the world—and herself—of how alluring she could be, and she was being darn successful at that.

"Is Vishwa in there too?" Anay asked.

"No," she said, her straight shoulder-length hair bouncing as she shook her head. "We were to have dinner but he didn't turn up."

"Oh..."

"I saw you with her. Your childhood friend. You aren't dropping her home or something?"

Anay sighed. He could hear many questions hidden within that one rhetorical interrogation. He said, "About that, Renee... see, she's a childhood friend. We just met each other all of a sudden and..."

"...sparks began to fly..."

"It's not like that, Renee. I mean, it could be but not yet. She doesn't feel the same way."

Renee took one long hard look at him. Then she shook her head. "Well, I don't care."

"Y-you don't?"

"Why should I?" she said. He realized she was drunk. "I mean, you have a great body and I'd like to be on top of it right now, but I'm no fool to think that you'll be only mine. Nor am I made to be for one person only. I don't believe in wasting this great body on only one bloke."

It was Anay's turn to stare at her. He then looked at his watch. In another half hour, it would be midnight. "So, should we book a cab like always?" he said. "Same direction and all?"

She nodded.

Anay busied himself with his phone. As he booked, he asked, "Why did Vishwa not turn up?"

"Let's not talk about that bastard. You know this is not the first time he has done this."

"But you waited too long for him. You probably came here hours ago..."

"Well, I had dressed up and all, so I thought I'd rather have a drink, after all," Renee said. "I spotted you guys an hour ago. You were discussing something important, or so it looked. So, I didn't bother you."

A cab stopped on the other side of the street. They crossed the street and got in.

Renee went on, "I don't know why I am such a sucker for him. I don't like him anymore. I mean, I have thought a hundred times to dump him, but it will get tricky. We work in the same office. I have a feeling he'll dump me first. Hallelujah if that happens."

Anay looked at her as she spoke. He was amazed at how pretty she looked. Renee had always been the flawless one, the one who woke up beautiful and got better as the day wore on, peaking at her most beautiful self at the night hour like this. A true queen of the night.

"Fuck it all, Anay... take me to your place," she said.

"What?" Anay said, shocked by the change in her tone.

"Why not? It's not like we haven't done stuff before. What has changed?"

"I don't know... I mean, I just met Shanaya and..."

"So it's okay if I can fuck you when I am with Vishwa, but you cannot do the same because now you are with some other girl? Don't worry anyway. You are not committed to her yet. You are not cheating on her."

Anay was blown away by that outright assessment. A part of his brain, the one governed by hormones, told him that was what he wanted to do. The night was long and lonely and with him was a beautiful woman making the first move.

"What do you say? You know a woman does not ask twice."

"Well, okay. Let's go."

They sat in near silence as the cab stopped by his building gate. He led her into the compound of the old building and got into the elevator. Her finger brushed against his and he felt his adrenaline beginning to pump. He led her to his house. As he thrust the key into the door of the apartment, the neighbor's door opened. Renee stepped back for no particular reason; she had nothing to hide from the neighbor.

"There was some mail for you in the evening," the elderly woman who stepped out of the neighbor's house told Anay. She had a couple of letters in her hand. Eying the girl behind him, she said, "Here they are."

"Oh yes... okay, thanks," said Anay as he grabbed them.

"Welcome. It is too much night. Have nice sleep," the woman said and popped inside her house.

Anay pushed the door of his house open and entered. Closing it behind Renee, he said, "Well, we are here."

"You certainly have creepy neighbors!" she said.

"Forget her," said Anay. "She is Mrs Shetty. Lonely elderly woman has little to look forward to in life. Holding on to the neighbor's mail and giving it to him is an adventure for her at this age."

She smiled and pulled him on the couch.

Anay let himself be led. "Let me at least turn on the lights..."

"Why? I am so turned on. Isn't that enough?"

He chuckled as her fingers worked their way on him.

Lost in the perfume of her hair, he let himself go with the moment. He kept his arms on the back of the couch and relaxed. Now and then, he felt like touching her, but somehow he could not will his hands to move to touch her. He looked at her head going down on him. In the darkness, all he could see of her was her straight silky blonde hair, dearly cared for at expensive salons. Then he felt her on him, and he almost lost consciousness.

But unknown to him, just a few feet away in the corner of the room at the far end, the one that was hidden away from the ambient streetlight that wafted into the room, something was happening. If he had stepped into that spot at that moment, he would have felt the shivering cold localized at that spot. Then, slowly, as if due to some invisible force, the air in that corner began to whirl, taking some of the dust particles with it. Noiselessly and invisibly, they swirled around, causing a sort of mini typhoon.

And from within that twister, something could see the two young people having the time of their lives. As they moaned and sighed, the wind began to spin faster, as if beset with some kind of fury. It then glided ahead, the bodiless entity shrouded within. It came out of the shadow of that corner and floated toward the partly bare bodies of the two people. It came behind the couch and stayed just behind Anay, barely grazing the nape of his neck and his shoulders.

Anay quickly turned to look. There was that feeling again. The cold, the darkness within the darkness. He could see nothing with his eyes, but his brain—oh, his brain! It conjured a million images, none of which he wanted to be true.

"Did you sense something?" he asked Renee.

She only grunted.

Just then, his phone rang and he jumped off the couch with a shriek.

"What the fuck, Anay? What's wrong with you?" Renee asked, almost falling off from her precarious position on her knees.

Anay gestured her to keep quiet. The call was from Shanaya. Turning his frown into a smile as if she could see him on the call, he cleared his throat and said, "Hi, Shan."

"Anay, I am feeling so bad about today, ya!" Shanaya said. "Look, I'm not a prude, but you know... we have just met. I like you. I like you very much, but let's just give it time, okay?"

Anay's attention was focused only on her voice; he paid scant attention to the words. His smile grew broader and he disconnected with "Sure! Let's talk tomorrow. Good night."

"What was that about?" Renee asked.

Anay now looked at the woman beside him. She was half-naked, in the middle of an act that he had been enjoying till just a moment ago but now found utterly despicable.

"It was Shanaya," he said truthfully.

"And she put a smile on your face, I see."

"It's okay, Renee. It's cool."

"No, it's not. How dare you take her call when I am here sucking your dick? What do you think I am?"

"Renee... it's not like that."

"Fuck you, Anay!" Renee fumed. "Seriously, fuck you! You are the biggest bastard I have ever met. I hope you go to hell."

"I'm sorry, Renee," Anay said, covering himself up. "I should have told you in the cab. Maybe you are right. I have feelings for her. And I am sorry I brought you home. I think this is not right. I cannot do this with Shanaya."

"The fuck do you mean? Am I a disposable condom to you?"

"I'm sorry. What can I do to make this right?"

Behind them, the swirling of the wind had stopped. The thing that was entrapped in it was now silent.

Renee rose and grabbed her clothes. She took her purse and furiously stormed to the door. "Never again cross paths with me, Anay Ghosh!" she screamed. "It won't be good."

Anay heard the door close with a bang. He then settled into the couch, a wry smile coming over his lips, thinking over what the woman of his fantasies had just told him on the phone.

Right behind him though, the blue eyes in that cloudy darkness blazed with a newfound rage.

Chapter 10

Mad as hell, Renee stomped out of the apartment in a blind rage. She muttered something to herself and repeated over and over that she had had it with men. Vishwa, Anay, they were all jerks. She waited a moment for the elevator, but she did not have the patience for it.

She took the stairs. They went around the side of the old building. The old design of the building had open windows that looked out into the compound below and the sea beyond. Much better for her present state of mind to let that sea breeze do its work and not stuff herself up in an elevator.

Renee grabbed the edge of the wall and walked quickly. Her clacking heels impeded her progress, and then there was all that booze and the pent-up rage within her. Men! She would never have a thing to do with men again if she could help it. They were all such bastards!

She descended the fourth floor and came to the third. At the head of the stairs, her high-heeled foot tripped. Wincing in pain and grabbing her foot, she screamed a loud expletive. She took another step down and stopped.

At the middle of the stairs, there was something.

She shivered. All of a sudden, the cold was immense. She stretched her arm and her fingers felt the icy coldness. What was wrong with that spot? Had something happened to the weather? She looked out of the window at the sea... There seemed to be nothing.

Slowly, as if someone spots a large unfriendly dog sleeping on the ground and tries to slide by sideways without waking him up, Renee tried to walk past that cold spot. If her compromised mind was right, there was something moving there. The staircase lighting of the old building was poor, but there was a darker patch, slightly bobbing up and down like a wavering cloth flag. She breathed hard, knowing instinctively to avoid whatever that was, and stepped to the very edge of the stairs, where the open window was.

A stitch of fear ran through her heart when she saw that thing move towards her.

And all of a sudden, it was on both sides of her, engulfing her in the middle.

She regretted her decision of not taking the elevator now. She turned to go back, back to the lobby of the third floor, or maybe even scoot to the fourth floor and ask Anay what the fuck this was, swallowing her pride, an act that she was no stranger to. But she could not turn. The thing was behind her too, flanking her on both sides, and when she tried to take one step towards it, it was like walking into a cascade of ice-cold sludge.

"Wh-what the fuck is this?" she said, trying to fish out her phone from her bag.

And in that moment, she heard something. A human voice, but she could not make out the words. Heck, she could not even tell if that voice was male or female. But there was that voice all right, and as she stared with her chest heaving into that black mass, she saw something materializing.

And it was a face!

It was a human face with wide staring eyes and mouth opened in a snarl. And those eyes! How horribly blue they were!

It was too much to take as that mouth breathed another gust of cold wind right at her. She recoiled in terror, and that was when she felt the stab of a cold fingertip on her chest, and that was all the force needed to topple backwards over the edge out of the window, hurtling down to the ground below.

Anay was still on the couch when he heard the piercing scream as it faded away to the depth of the building. He rushed to look out of the window of his house, and he lost his senses when he saw the body thudding on the ground. The next moment, Renee was spattered on the ground, her limbs broken and twisted at an obscene angle. Her eyes were still open. She saw him in the window for a brief heart-stopping moment, tried to say something, and then writhing in maddening agony, she turned deathly still.

CHAPTER 11

It was like a mindless reverie playing out.

Anay was in some kind of fugue state, with no sense of what was going on around him. There were people around him everywhere, talking in loud angry voices, but he had little sense of who they were. Everything was a blur, a distorted spectrum of crazy colors dancing beyond the spots in front of his eyes.

Somewhere above him, there was that booming voice again: "Tell me, asshole, what was that girl doing in your house so late in the night?"

There was a crack of something over his head. He turned his head to see even crazier lights, and cutting through those lights was the distended silhouette of something long, and he realized instantly what it was—a policeman's baton.

He gained some consciousness. He was on the floor of the police station. There was a stench all around him, that of dusty furniture and molding walls and crumbling paper files. He could see the policemen's khaki clad legs and their leather boots. He was not given a chair to sit on. He was made to squat in a corner on the floor surrounded by the rank odor of shoes and socks of the uniforms around him. His dank perspiration made his shirt cling to his body. He hated every bit of what was happening. He hated himself too, but he had no control over it. He had lost control the moment the police had banged on his door in the middle of the night. They had claimed to have a statement from his neighbor, Ratna Shetty, who had stated that the poor deceased girl had entered the house with him. Even that would have been all right, but Shetty, in her zeal, had shared with the police that she had overheard an altercation between the boy and the girl and her death might not have been an accident.

The inspector, whose tag pronounced his name as B. Sawant, tapped the baton on his shoulder. "We know she didn't die by accident. Nobody falls off a building just like that. Cooperate with us and you will be happier."

Anay cried out loud, "There's nothing to say, sir! She is... was a friend. We spent time together, our group of friends."

Sawant made a throaty sound. "Fucker, do you recognize me? I spoke to you at the café that day. Aren't you the selfish bastard who did not save that poor café owner's life when you could have? So now you have graduated to murder?"

"Sir!"

"Why was that girl in your house at that indecent hour?"

"Sir..." Anay fumbled for words. Over his head, he heard the obscene sniggering of the policemen.

"Was she your girlfriend?" Sawant asked.

"No, sir."

"Oh, so she was... what do you guys call it? Fuck buddy?" More sniggering followed.

"We were just chilling, sir."

"Fucker! I know what that means. Don't think I am a baby," Sawant boomed. "What happened then? Did she refuse to suck your dick? Did you have a fight?"

"No, sir."

"Bastard! Let me tell you what I think. You brought your friend home. Both of you were drunk. A lot. You wanted a good time, of course, and she did not agree. So you tried to rape her."

"NO, SIR!" Anay screamed in anger, rising on his feet.

That same instant, his body was impinged by a bolt of electricity. It took a moment for him to realize what had happened—a constable had hit on his knee hard with the baton. Anay crashed on the floor, grabbing his knee, writhing. "Motherfucker!" he yelled. But the constable, immune to all abuse, only kicked him harder and prodded him into the humiliating squatting position again.

The inspector continued his theory oblivious to his reaction, "But then she tried to run away. You got scared that she might complain about you. So you followed her and pushed her off the building in your mad impulse."

Watching the constable's baton nervously, Anay said, "No, sir. Nothing like that happened. It was an accident."

Sawant snorted. Going down on his haunches, he stared into Anay's perspiring face. "Do you think I am a fool?" he said, spittle flying out of his mouth. "We checked the height of that window. It's not so low that anyone could just fall off it."

Anay held the inspector's gaze. He had to find the courage within himself to come out of this ordeal. "I am not a roadside goon, sir," he said in a calm but unwavering voice. "I am an employee at a respectable company. I am well-educated management degree holder."

Maybe it was that last statement that provoked the inspector. Without any warning, he landed a firm slap across his cheek, so hard that Anay toppled over on the ground.

"Flaunting your education at me, you bastard! Shove your degrees up your ass!" he yelled.

"You cannot hit me!" Anay shouted back. "I know my rights. I am not a criminal."

Fire arose in the inspector's eyes. "You cock-sucking son of a whore! You will teach me what to do? I've had enough of assholes like you migrating here from other cities under the pretext of work and then raping our girls." Turning to his constable, he said, "Strip this fucker naked and dump him in the lockup for the night. Let me see if I cannot kill his pride."

Anay knew it was illegal. The inspector had taken a dislike to him at first sight, and that made things all the more complicated. There ought to be something he could do, but what? He was alone. Who could he have reached out to? In a flash, he thought of all the possibilities. Salil, perhaps. But how could he talk to him? And no, what was he thinking! Salil must not know. Salil was his boss. He'd not want a jail-stained fellow in his company. Could he call Vishwa or Kautuk? No, then Vishwa would know. He'd be in a boiling rage when he found out that Renee was with him... Then who? Shanaya, perhaps?

He felt the constable's hand on his neck. He was lifted off the ground with that force and marched to the back of the police station where the lockups were. Even in his half-conscious state, he could see the people in the lockup. Petty criminals all, kept in the lockup as a temporary measure, only for a scare perhaps. There'd never be a trial, for they would be released by morning. He imagined being put in there with them. Would he be the same man in the morning?

He heard the constable ordering him to strip. "Didn't you hear, fucker? Sir has asked you to get naked."

There was a leery shout from the cells. A gruff heavily-bearded man tugged at his crotch obscenely. Others jeered. Anay trembled in fear and embarrassment. He would be their entertainment for the night.

"This is not right," Anay said, his tears choking him.

The constable laughed and the criminals followed. "In this place, whatever Sawant says is right!" he declared.

The baton was raised again, this time aimed for his other knee. Tears rolling down his cheeks, Anay unbuttoned his shirt and let it drop. The occupants of the lockup cheered him on with their derisive hoots and abuses. The constable pointed his baton at his belt. He let his pants drop, leaving his briefs on. More jeering followed. Someone passed a comment. He felt like an object in a cage. His vision blurred. He felt the baton's tip on his waist, egging him on to remove the last bit of clothing.

Just as Anay was about to succumb to the ultimate humiliation, he heard a voice outside. For a moment, he could not believe his ears. Then he smiled and took away his finger from the waistband of his briefs. It was Kautuk arguing with the inspector.

"You cannot do this, Inspector, and you know that," Kautuk was saying in a firm no-nonsense voice. "My friend is not a criminal. You can question him but not humiliate him. My uncle is a criminal lawyer with the High Court. Naresh Tiwari. Look him up. I know the law. You have to let my friend go right now."

A few moments later, Anay was marched out again, back to Sawant's busy desk. Sawant looked at him as if he were a worm. "I am allowing you to go now, motherfucker," he said, "but we will be meeting again very soon. Be assured of that."

Anay walked out. He did not look at Kautuk's bewildered expression at his disarrayed state. They hardly spoke. Kautuk took him to a waiting cab and brought him to his apartment. It was dawn when they reached.

Chapter 12

Anay woke up to find Kautuk on his bed next to him. He sat up and suddenly looked at his miserable state. He still felt naked and humiliated; he felt touched. Visuals of the harrowing experience at the police station with the groggy criminals' eyes leering at him danced in front of his eyes. Kautuk stirred and snored. Anay thought of waking him up but knowing that the guy had been out for him the entire night, he let him sleep.

He walked to the bathroom, suddenly alive to the many places that his body had started to ache in. Standing in front of his mirror, he looked at the bruise on the corner of his lip. It was a reminder of the slap. He kept his foot on the commode with great difficulty and looked at his knee. It was bruised blue. He would be stumbling for a few days. He applied an ointment and winced as it burned through the sore skin. But then another visual sprang to his mind with the momentum of a runaway truck—the thought of the poor dead body of Renee on the ground of the building, that was there just a few hours ago. In a blink, it obliterated every other thought from his mind.

He washed his face and hobbled up to the balcony. He leaned out and could see the chalk outline drawn by the police on the ground below. The corpse was gone but the bloodstains were there. Two constables were sitting at the building gate. They had perhaps been stationed for the final formalities. Just then, they looked up and saw him at the window. He hastily retreated into the room and closed the window with a bang.

Kautuk stirred and sat up. "Fuck, is it eleven already?" was the first thing he said.

Anay came up to him. "Thank you, buddy. How can I ever thank you? If it were not for you..." That thought remained unspoken, but it played out in his mind and his voice broke.

Kautuk let his friend's emotions flow. He lit a cigarette, blew a puff, and handed it over to Anay. "Have it. You'll feel better." Anay took a long drag. Staring at him, Kautuk said, "I knew Renee and you were up to something. That blind fool Vishwa could not see it, but nothing escapes me. Now tell me exactly what happened."

"I don't know, man!" Anay said. "Yes, we came up here to the house. No, it wasn't a plan. She just met me and then we came up here together. It was all her idea. You cannot blame me. You know how Renee can get when she needs something. She was all over me."

"And then?"

"Well, I couldn't do it. I really couldn't. I told her so. And then she got wild. She called me all sorts of names and ran out of the house, slamming the door behind her. That was the last I saw of her."

"You didn't run behind her?"

"Nope. I was, in a way, happy that she left." Anay buried his head in his hands.

Kautuk placed his arm on Anay's shoulder. "Look, brother. I trust you. I spoke to my lawyer uncle before coming over. He has represented some of the biggest criminals in town and got them acquitted. This one will be a breeze for him. Apart from that woman's statement, the police have nothing. My will get you out of this and you'll not even know. Just stay put."

Anay nodded. "How did you know?"

"Well, the police called Vishwa as soon as they found her body. Vishwa called me up and asked me if I knew anything about Renee being here, in your house. He didn't even seem to register that she is dead. He was only going on and on about 'Why was she in his house?'"

"So Vishwa knows?"

"Vishwa knows."

"And what about Salil? I need to get back to work."

"Take it easy for a couple of days," Kautuk said. "Salil surely knows about it by now. He'll understand."

"But the project, man… I promised Sen a week."

"An employee of our firm has died. If Sen has a single human bone in his body, he'll understand. If he does not, you'll be happier to not be associated with him anymore."

Anay buried his face in his palms. "My life is fucked, man! Someone is trying to screw up my life. It's that same thing that has been stalking me. Fuck that cocksucker! Everything was going so right…"

"All will be well," said Kautuk, patting his friend on the shoulder. "There is some bad luck in your life right now, but we will sort it out."

There was a long spell of silence. Kautuk did not refer to his previous conversation, though the allusion of 'bad luck' had been made. Those two words remained hanging in the air even after he left.

In the late afternoon, there was a wild knocking on the door.

Anay, who had dozed off again after Kautuk left, woke up with a spasm. He realized it wasn't a nightmare. There was someone at the door, someone very pissed off by the way they were thumping at it.

Terror coursing through him again, Anay crept cautiously to the door and opened it.

Before he could see who it was, a hand flew at his throat. Angry words fell upon him like rapid fire, "You bastard motherfucker! Why did you do this to my daughter? Why?"

Anay blinked his eyes to see. It was Joaquim Pinto, Renee's father. He had met him only once when Renee had taken him to talk to him about finding accommodation. Behind him was Mukesh Patel, the owner of the house he was renting.

"I didn't do anything, Mr Pinto! It was an accident," Anay said with a shudder.

"But she was here in your house. Why?"

"It was her idea, sir."

"And you got carried away. What are you, a six-year-old?"

Anay stepped back, fearing an assault. "Mr Pinto, please hear me out."

"No. I will not. I will not give you that chance. I am sure the police are dealing with you," Pinto said, staring at his torn lip. "I hope they hang you from the highest noose. You killed my delicate child." He sat down on the bed, breaking down into profuse tears.

Anay did not know what to say. He flinched at the sight of a grown man crying thus. There was no way he could imagine the sorrow and anger the man felt at that moment. Anay realized that.

The landlord stepped forward. "Young man, I have come to tell you to pack your stuff and clear out of here by tomorrow morning."

Now, Anay's world spun around him. All at once, he realized the import of those words. "No, Mr Patel, please don't do that!" he said, falling at his feet in an extreme reflex action. "I have not done anything, sir. Renee's death was just an accident. My name will clear out soon, I promise."

"Don't you dare take my daughter's name with your filthy mouth!" Pinto screamed and landed a full-blown slap right across Anay's face.

Anay was stunned. It felt as if his bearings had come loose. That was the slap of man who was livid with rage and sadness. It hit like an explosion.

"It's not just about her," Anay heard Patel's words over the ringing in his ears. "I thought you were a decent boy. I cannot allow this kind of thing. You are bringing girls to my house. What will I tell the society members? This is a decent society; people with families live here. All my friends told me not to rent my apartment to a single young man. Pinto, if it were not for your request... Anyway, young man, get out of my house by morning." He turned to Pinto. "Pinto, come on. We have to make the arrangements for the funeral of our little girl."

Pinto broke into a loud wail and he turned to the door, his mind relapsing to an unconscious wrap. Anay tried to beseech, to implore, to make them see reason despite their mourning, but it was to no avail.

The men left the house and, that very moment, the door slammed shut with a deafening noise. Anay looked at it, speechless. He knew instantly that there was something behind that slamming. It hadn't happened because of any natural reason. Then, his fears were confirmed. Standing by the door, he saw a hazy misty figure, a figure looming large over him, its bright blue eyes the only thing clear and visible. Then it disappeared but left behind in its wake was the unbearable sound of a faint chuckle.

Anay screamed out loud, "Are you happy with how you are screwing my life, motherfucker?"

His words echoed in the empty apartment, but Anay knew someone had heard, for the laughing still continued in his ears.

Anay did not know for how long he had been lying on the floor. His mind was inundated with thoughts, which, like a medley of ghosts refused to leave him. He thought of Salil, who must be fuming as well. The project was as good as gone. Maybe his job too. His name was tarnished because of no fault of his. And he was suddenly homeless. The feeling of loneliness had increased a hundredfold. Who did he have that he could call his own? He remembered the many cautions from his family members that the city would eat him up, that he would find himself alone with no support whatsoever, and it was probably coming true. But, now, where would he go? Could he go back to his family home? He remembered the miserable way in which he had gotten away from there to come to the city. Would they accept him back? Would he be able to live down the humiliation of it even if they did?

The devil had succeeded in his mission of wrecking his life. For some reason, the devil had made him his marked child, and his blessings were curses. It was probably his karma that had brought the devil to him. That was all it was about; what else could it be?

Everything that he had until yesterday had been snatched away. A young confident chap who was ready to take on the world had now been reduced to a beggar dependent on the mercies of other people. What had brought him to this?

That talk of bad luck, it came back to him. It had been playing on his mind. He could feel it now too. It was in the air around him, that thick black aura that was threatening him. It was drawing closer and closer upon him, and he did not know what it was. The face of Shanaya loomed in his mind, but he did not dare to entertain her even in a vision. What if the devil saw her in his imaginations and targeted her as well? Or was she a lure sent by the devil to him? Was she really a jinx for him? Not having the courage to face her, he had kept his cellphone switched off the entire day.

From his position on the floor, he looked at the balcony window outside the apartment, the apartment that he would soon leave. He had spent many nights in that balcony, just smiling at the good turns of his fortune. Those good turns were gone, and now the balcony would go as well. Everything drifting away, like a memory and nothing more.

Somehow, he stood up, bearing heavily on his still-throbbing knee, and came into the balcony. It had turned evening already. He hadn't even realized how the hours had passed. He lit up another cigarette and stood there. He could not see the police constables. There were the security guards and they were talking to some of the senior residents of the building. Now and then, they looked up at his window, leaving no doubt of the topic of discussion. He was a criminal without a crime.

That chalk outline was still there like an indelible stain, drawing his attention. Poor, poor Renee! She had been so alive just a few hours ago, a girl filled with passions and aspirations, and now she was nothing but a few bloodstains on the ground. Those vestiges of death stirred something in his soul. The blackness consumed his completely. It rose from his innards and grabbed his throat, choking him, making him realize the futility of fighting. There was no fight in him left.

His life was a long black tunnel without a way out.

Or perhaps there was a way out.

As he looked at that chalk outline, he saw that way out.

Yes. That was the only way out…

He snuffed out the half-smoked cigarette under his bare foot, and he didn't even wince at the burn. His eyes were only on that outline now. In a flash, he saw Renee there again, writhing and squirming, and then she paused and looked right at him and smiled with her bloody teeth. "Come," she said through her smashed jaw. "Come to me, Anay. You can do it. Just a moment of pain and then freedom from all this misery."

Drowned in his stupor, Anay could think of nothing else, or see nothing else. He placed one foot on the railing of his balcony and then another. He was now up there, perched precariously on his balcony ledge, four stories above the hard unforgiving concrete ground below, tearfully prepared to dive to his doom and end it all.

Chapter 13

A senior man who was chatting up with the security guards at the building gate was the one to see him first.

Blinking against the growing darkness of the sunset, the man hollered, "Hey! What is that boy doing? Oh God, is he trying to jump out of his window?"

Suresh Oza, the retired banker, was a father of three sons, all of whom were settled outside the country. He had all the time in the world to talk about issues that did not matter to him. Gossiping about an alleged murder by that debauched single man living on the fourth floor of the E wing was the kind of thing that he and his group of retirees were happy to talk about. But the man trying to kill himself by suicide was a twist in the tale that was hard to take even for him.

"Do something, guard! Save the man!" Oza shouted.

The guard fumbled. "What can I do, sir?" Turning to Anay up in his window, the guard blew his whistle hard and waved his hands, "Sir, get down, sir. You will fall!"

"Idiot, that's precisely what he's trying to do," Oza screamed at the guard.

Another guard left his post and ran up to the building in a bid to reach the fourth floor as quickly as possible. More people gathered below. A group of boys in the park left their game of football and came to watch this more interesting show.

For Anay up there, everything was a blur. How long would they shout? How long would he hear them? In a few seconds, no noise would ever be able to reach him.

"You cannot do this, young man!" Oza shouted as if it was a rule he had laid down. "You cannot end it like this. Be a brave man and face the consequences."

Face the consequences?

"I have done nothing!" Anay shouted angrily, not sure who he was trying to convince.

Oza looked at the gathered crowd and shook his head helplessly. "The youth of today," he told the people loud enough for Anay to hear. "First they do such things and then they cannot face it even."

That was it! Anay shut his eyes and shut out all the noise. No one could reach him. He cut out those horrid visuals of the screaming guards and the old man and everyone else, and of the chalk outline that he was going to meet soon. Perched on the balcony ledge with his feet curled around it and his hands outstretched, he looked much like a diver ready to take the plunge.

People gasped. The shouting increased. There was banging on his door, trying to break it down. The watchman had evidently reached.

Anay shut his eyes and began to count in his mind...

"Five...four...three..."

He felt like a free bird. He saw the pain going away. He gathered his last ounce of courage...

"two...one..."

It was at that exact moment that something most incredible happened.

He felt a grip around his waist. It was as if someone had a tight hold of him at the waist. It was a firm grip, kind of a wrestler's hold. He could feel the musculature of the palms of the hands and, as he was hoisted in the air, he was aware that whoever it was that had grabbed him was blessed with a great deal of strength. Before he could open his eyes and see who the person was, he was pulled back into the balcony and dropped on the floor. Anay screamed in agony as his back crashed against the floor of his balcony. He hadn't just been dropped; it was as if he had been flung in anger. And as if that was not enough, the next moment, he experienced a strong gust of wind. It was so strong indeed that it swept him back into the house with great speed and that was where he crashed and landedbacked up against the wall of the house.

He understood nothing. For a moment he thought he had died and this was the bizarre part of his afterlife where he was seeing things that did not exist. But it was the pain on his head and his back that made him realize that he was not dead. Afterlife cannot be so painful.

And there was one more thing that punctuated the fact that he was not dead.

It was a shadow billowing over him now, the shadow that had snatched him away from his death. It looked ghastly but at the same time there was in it the sense of accomplishment of having saved his life. And then, even as he looked at that curling smoke-like apparition with its blazing blue eyes, he heard a single sentence spoken with the uttermost ominousness:

"You will die when I am done with you..."

Anay's bones chilled at that voice. There was such menace in it, such rancor! This thing, whatever it was, hated him to the guts. What was this thing, which had made his life miserable and death impossible? Why could it not show itself to him clearly? What infernal sorcery was this?

"Who are you?" he asked, convulsing with a mix of emotions. "Why are you after my life?"

Upon that, the entity made a noise and retreated back into the shadows.

Those words would not leave him though. He could not tell whose voice it was. It did not sound human. It was a ghastly bestial disembodied voice that left a ringing tone in his ears and made them pop. It made his eardrums run cold and he felt accursed just for having heard it. But his brain told him something else. It told him, in that wise sage-like manner that only a few of us can bear, that he had heard that voice before. He was not a stranger to it.

It was late evening when Anay stepped out of the building with two suitcases. It astounded him as to how few his belongings were. How easy it had been for him to pack everything he had in two travel bags and just walk away!

For one last time, he looked at Renee's outline on the ground. Up close, it was more harrowing. Leaving his bags, he walked up to the spot and stood in meditation and said a little prayer. Prayer. There hadn't been one on his lips since a long time. Perhaps it was time to reflect on that too and not take his blessings for granted.

Oza was still on the park bench, stretching his rheumatic legs. When he saw Anay, he rose with some effort and walked up to him.

"Leaving?" he said. "I hope Patel has your forwarding address. We don't want the police to pester us here."

Anay did not respond.

"Good that you are moving," the old man continued. "At least you are showing some responsibility towards the building. Young man, you are my youngest son's age. Mend your ways. All this philandering feels good for a while but, trust me, it can ruin your life. But why am I telling you this? You are already experiencing it."

Anay wished there were a way to shut the old man up.

"And what was that foolishness you were doing up there? Trying to jump out of the window. Do you think it would have earned you any sympathy? You'd just have become another stain on the ground. And think of your parents, wherever they are. But why would you think? Your generation is a useless selfish generation. It is good that your friend pulled you back into the house in the nick of time, or"

Now Anay paid attention. "My friend? Did you see who pulled me back into the house?"

Oza eyed him as if he were a specimen from outer space. "Have you gone completely mad? Of course, I saw him..."

Anay, forgetting who he was talking to, shook the man by his shoulders in excitement. "Uncle, please tell me who he was. Are you sure he was a man? How did he look? Tell me. Tell me, please."

"What nonsense is this!" Oza screamed. "Take your hands off me, young man."

Anay backed off. "I'm sorry. But I want to know who it was."

"Are you out of your mind? He was in your house and you don't know who he was?"

"Was it a he?"

Oza reflected. "I'm almost sure. But no, I don't know. Your generation dresses up so confusingly; it's hard to tell. Are you playing some funny game"

"Young or old?"

"Young. Definitely young."

"Could you see him? I mean, his features?"

"Thin guy. Not taller than you. He had thick glasses on his eyes, that much is for sure. He crept up from behind you and grabbed you when you were in that crazy chicken posture on the ledge. That's all I saw."

Anay shook. There was someone. This was the strongest validation of it he had had. Not only had a crowd of people seen him but he had felt his grip too. It appeared to others in the form of a man but to him in the form of a horrific spirit. Which was his true form, then? He looked up at that house and shuddered. He prayed hard that that thing stayed in that damned house and did not follow him, whatever it was.

Kautuk came running downstairs when Anay entered his compound in a cab. He got into the cab and said, "I spoke to someone. He's a friend, a man named Pradhan. He owns a motel near the highway, and you can stay there for a few days. There will be traffic noise. But it's off-season and he will ask you no questions."

"Thanks, man!" Anay said. "Does he know about my situation?"

"He knows you have been kicked out of your apartment."

"And the other thing? About... about the police?"

"Don't worry. He owes me. Guys and middle-aged businessmen take girls there over the weekends for a quick screw. He deals in shady stuff all the time. I have sent a lot of guests to his motel. Friends from my college and their girlfriends. All kinds of things go on there. All kinds of people come there. But you stay put in your room and you'll be fine. I hope you have your identification with you."

Anay checked his back pocket and nodded.

"Meanwhile, my uncle will handle everything about the, you know, police thing. It will tide over soon, buddy."

Anay's eyes began to overflow with tears, a sensation that he had rarely experienced in his life. It is true, perhaps, that even when everything is going wrong, there is that one something, that one flickering flame, that keeps things going. For him, it was this guy, Kautuk. The guy who he had always dismissed as a kind of clown was the one who was coming to his aid now.

"I will forever be indebted to you, Kautuk," he said, and proceeded to hug him.

Kautuk, somewhat surprised, received the hug. Then he withdrew almost immediately. "It's okay. What are friends for?" he asked.

Anay had no words. For several minutes, they were in silence. Then Anay thought of something, made a resolve, and said, "Kautuk bro, something weird happened in the house just before I was leaving it."

"What?"

Anay launched into a full-fledged description of the episode that had unfolded. He kept some details to himself, such as his attempt to end his life. Keeping a careful eye on the driver, he filtered out some of the ghostly details too, so that the cabdriver did not think of him as a madman.

Kautuk heard it all in silence. Anay ended his narration with the description Oza had given him. Kautuk raised his brows. "The old man really saw someone?"

"That's what everyone has been telling me, bro. And today..." Anay lowered his voice. "...I actually felt him grab me and heard his voice. See, right here." He lifted his shirt to show his midriff. "I can still feel his cold grip."

"This is very strange," Kautuk said, feeling the faint black marks on Anay's waist with the tips of his fingers. "I have heard of houses being haunted, but this is the first time I am actually seeing someone go through it. Well, isn't it nice that you are out of that house?"

"Kautuk, I am sure this is the same thing that pushed Renee off the building. I now know he has a strong physical hold. This is not a simple ghost or apparition."

Kautuk opened his mouth to say something and then clamped up. He said instead, "Then you are fucked."

"What? Why?"

"Well, even my genius uncle wouldn't be able to prove in court that a ghost committed the murder."

There were no more words spoken in the car. As Anay sat as if in shock, Kautuk squeezed his thigh in reassurance. "Hang in there, buddy. Everything will be all right," he said.

Chapter 14

The first thing Anay did after settling at the motel, even before looking around to see if it was livable, was to make a call to Shanaya. He tried not to look at the many missed calls from her and he did not even check his messages because he knew there would be a flood of them; he directly called.

She answered on the first ring. "Where are you, Anay? I have been so worried."

"Shan, listen... a lot of things have happened."

"Like what?"

"Not on the phone. Let's meet."

"Cool. Where are you? In the office?"

"Haven't gone to office for three days."

"Why? Are you ill?"

"Nothing as simple as that. But I'll tell you. Look, I have moved from the Versova apartment. I am in Mira Road now."

There was a moment of stunned silence, and then she said, "That far? Overnight?"

"I will come to you."

"The Bandana? Tonight?"

Anay shook his head. "No. Too many memories there. Let me message you the location of another smaller place."

"You are scaring me, Anay."

Without replying to that, he disconnected the phone.

He met her in the evening at Village Shack, a small eatery by the Versova beachside. It was close to his previous apartment. As he went past it in the cab, he saw the dark balcony of it, looking all the more ominous. It was all a bit unsettling, but he didn't want to put Shanaya too much out of the way. When he saw her enter the restaurant with an intense frown on that pretty forehead and still looking like an angel who had somehow landed on earth, he knew that the trip was worth it.

She rushed to him as soon as she spotted him. He ordered the food right away, even the main course, for he did not want to be disturbed by the waiter midway during his narration. Then he opened the conversation, and, for the next two hours, he told her about his terrible mistake of taking Renee home, her death, his tryst at the police station, and his subsequent removal from the house. What he did not tell her—rather, carefully hid from her—was any mention of the inexplicable things that happened in the house. He wanted to tell her but at the very moment, the words just froze in his mouth. How could he tell her that a ghost had killed Renee? She'd probably upturn the glass of cold water on his head, call him a loon, and walk out of the place. He had shocked her enough anyway.

"Oh my God, Anay!" she said at last, letting out a long breath from her pursed lips. "So much happened in two days? So much? And Renee? Wasn't that the girl who I met at the office? Is the poor thing really dead?"

Anay nodded.

"How?"

"It was an accident, Shanaya. Our building staircase has open walls."

"But that's fucking irresponsible of your building authorities. The builder or whoever is concerned must be arrested. Why did they come to you?"

"Because she was in my house, that's why. Our neighbor heard us having an argument. I was picked up for questioning."

Shanaya opened her mouth to say something and then let it pass. It was clear she wanted to ask about why Renee was in the house, but for some reason she thought better of it.

"It's not what you think," Anay said. "Renee and I just used to… chill out sometimes. Just casual, Shanaya. There was no emotion attached to it on either side."

"Did you have sex?"

"At times," he said and looked into his plate. Shanaya did not reply but Anay could read her mind. He could read the accusation. She probably wanted to call him out on being so horny that soon after being turned down by her, he found the next available skirt. "Shanaya, it is true that I took her up to my house," he said in a voice that one uses when confessing their sins to a pastor in a church. "But, believe me, it was she who insisted. Even then, I did nothing. She wanted to do a lot of things but I could not respond."

"Why?"

"I don't know." He could not tell Shanaya that he was thinking of her.

"And then?"

"Renee got mad at me and stormed out of the house. That was the last I saw of her."

Shanaya stayed quiet for a long moment. Then she said in a low voice, "Somehow, Anay, I think I am responsible for her death too."

"What nonsense? Why do you say that?"

"You asked me first. If I had gone with you to your house, Renee would not have happened at all."

Anay lowered his head into his plate. "That's actually a stupid thing to think. The way things are going on in my life, I am sure even that would not have been a good idea." He almost told her about his mysterious ghost stalker but could not. If he did, she'd definitely think he was a fool and leave her. Anyway, it didn't matter anymore—he told himself. He was out of that goddammed house.

"Screw it all! Let's go catch a movie," he said all of a sudden.

Shanaya laughed with a mouthful of food. "What?"

"Yes, I need some cheering up. There's this unforgivably cheesy movie playing right now. Let's go and lose a few more hours of this shitty life." He rose from his chair.

"Wait! Let me at least finish the food."

"Hurry up, Shan! We can still make the 8.30 show."

Chapter 15

They had just enough time to grab the tickets at the box office and run into the auditorium. The movie had completed a run of two weeks already and was now on the way out. It was the middle of a busy week, and, as expected, they walked into a near-empty auditorium that was already plunged in darkness.

"What are the seat numbers?" Shanaya asked.

"Sit anywhere. What does it matter?" He indicated two seats in the corner of the third-last row. There were people in the last three rows, and a few heads were spread out in the lower rows. The third row, however, was empty. He led Shanaya to the very end of the row and sat next to her.

"I wanted to do something fun with you but didn't know it would be sudden like this!" Shanaya said.

"Well, what do I tell you? I am an impulsive guy," Anay said and hailed an usher who was on his way out and bought a tub of caramel popcorn.

"What's the movie about?" Shanaya asked.

"Who cares?" he said and they laughed.

The movie began to play. It started with a riveting opening scene with the introduction of the main character—a loser who was being dumped by his girlfriend. In the first seven minutes, it was clear that this was a typical movie where the loser would suddenly grow balls and stop a burning train or something and then prove his worth to his girlfriend. The movie wasn't expected to have the IQ level for a story more layered than that, but in that moment, Anay was moved. That loser, that miserable sod who couldn't get anything right, was he.

Around half an hour into the movie, Anay realized that Shanaya's hand was grazing his on the armrest. She was probably unaware of it, but that was suddenly all that he could think of. Who was he kidding anyway? Girls don't do anything without their knowledge. They are just not biologically equipped to be unaware of their surroundings. He looked at her and he was right. She gave him a brief look out of the corners of her eyes and then she took her hand away. He breathed hard.

"Popcorn?" he asked her, suddenly remembering he had them.

"No, they get stuck in my teeth."

"What a shame!" He sat back in his seat, tucking the overlarge popcorn bucket in the space between his legs and began to dig in. It was good that the movie was noisy—lots of cars exploding for no particular reason—and that the hall was near-empty; his ungodly crunching of the popcorn did not bother anyone.

Anay had, all of a sudden, lost all interest in the movie. Shanaya was definitely enjoying it, but he was trying hard to. He kept his arm on the armrest, hoping that she would keep hers again, but that did not happen. At one point, he began to feel drowsy. It was perhaps the sleeplessness of the past many nights that was getting to him. His eyes began to droop.

And then suddenly he looked up at the screen. But where was the screen? It was not a cinema screen. It was something dark, something ungodly. It was a kind of theater stage, and something was going on there—the preparation for a play, perhaps? Strange exaggerated characters dressed in colorful clothes flitted across the stage. They wore eerie makeup and even eerier smiles on their faces. He looked around, breathing hard, and saw that he was alone. Those horrific people on stage were performing only for him. A song was playing somewhere, a kind of a lullaby designed to put one into permanent sleep, and somehow he knew that song was only for him. His head began to churn; the people on stage blended with each other and there was a whirlpool of colors, and he felt sucked in at the vortex. He felt his life being squeezed out, whatever there was of it, and then, in a flash, it was all gone. He was alert again. The ridiculous movie was back on the screen.

He shook himself awake from that horrible nightmare. But what was that about? It was as if he had entered into some retro sepia world from the past, like he had flitted across time dimensions, and was back. He shook himself trying to ward off the vestiges of that horrible dream.

Everyone in the cinema hall laughed loudly at some joke that played out in the movie. Anay took a sip from the water bottle he had wedged in the seat slot.

Trying to focus on the movie now, he remembered that he had the popcorn. He thrust his hand into it and grabbed a few. He wasn't drowsy anymore. He looked at the screen, trying to follow the movie. It was a romantic scene between the main characters. A man and a woman were out on the street on a rainy night for some reason. The screen was dark; he had to squint to see and follow.

He went a few times at the popcorn and then his hand brushed against another soft hand in the bucket.

He smiled.

Suddenly happy and aware of her lavender fragrance, he retreated. He allowed her to take some of the popcorn and then said, "I thought you didn't like popcorn."

She didn't say anything, concentrating too hard at the romantic scene. He did not want to break her concentration. Let her get into the mood, he said to himself.

He absorbed himself into the movie again then, continuing to have the popcorn along with, seeing how the woman on screen was reaching out for the man's lips. He waited for her hand to come into the popcorn bucket again. And when it did, he did not pull his hand out. Their hands wriggled in the bucket for a few seconds before she pulled it out. And then they did it again.

It was now a game that was more enjoyable to him than the movie on the screen. He played with those fingers, and at one point, he thrust his long finger into the gap between her fingers and stroked it suggestively. She did not flinch.

Then the game became a bit bolder.

Her hand moved away from the popcorn bucket and traveled a few inches upward. He didn't dare to look down, for what if he embarrassed her and she withdrew her hand? But he could almost not breathe now, conscious of every centimeter that her fingers were moving up, and then a huge grin erupted on his lips as the fingers brushed against the fabric of his jeans. He relaxed and stretched his legs. He had been bearing that agony for a while now. Her hand in the popcorn bucket wedged between his legs had been teasing him, arousing him, and he hadn't been so aroused in a while, and now it was happening. It was really happening!

"Shan," he breathed her name and shut his eyes as he felt her fingers squeezing his unbearable hardness and they did that for a while, almost persistently, and then those fingers pushed upwards along his zipper and slipped into his shirt to play with the hair under his navel. They groped in an attempt to locate the button of his jeans. The theater was absolutely dark, and the nearest person was sitting several rows away. Shamelessly grinning at the prospect of what was going to happen, Anay moved to assist those delicate fingers groping him. He unbuttoned his jeans and sat with his arms on the head of his seat, letting her do what she wanted to. What he wanted to.

Her hand went right through the waistband of his briefs. Oh fuck! Was this real? He thanked his stars, he thanked the darkness of the hall, he thanked the popcorn, he thanked everything! He wanted to touch her too, and he wanted to do it so bad, but he desisted. What if she became conscious and pulled away?

It was the first time that he was feeling her like this. It was a moment of great joy, a memorable moment to cherish. Perhaps it was the resumption of the good things in his life. One good thing can obliterate a chain of jinxes. That was what was happening. The cloud of doom over his head was lifting. And to think he had thought, even though fleetingly, that she was the bad luck in his life. If anything, she would remove any ill luck his fate had in store for him.

His eyes still shut, he groaned. She was good at it. Undoubtedly. Her fingers, comfortably cold with all the air-conditioning, were the right mix of gentle touch and firm pressure. But he wanted her too. He could not just take. He had to give as well. Hell, he wanted to give! The boyhood kiss jumped back into his memory and he wanted it again. He wanted those lips on his and his tongue in her mouth, and he thought of how their smooth tongues would lock with each other, sliding up and down, copulating of their own accord. All caution be damned, he had the tremendous urge to kiss her. And then do more.

Maybe fuck the movie and take her home. She wouldn't refuse now, would she?

He leaned forward in her direction, his lips puckered, and was just about to hold her chin with his hand, when he opened his eyes.

And he froze.

Shanaya was watching the movie with great interest, completely immersed in it, her attention totally on what was going on there. Her hands—both her hands—were in a tight fold across her chest, and she was even mouthing the lines of dialog. Her attention was not on him at all!

Then...who was it? Whose hand was on his cock, which he could still feel? That touch, it was so alive, so real! Whose touch was it?

Horrified, he looked down at his crotch. There was nothing. No hands had been touching him. Only, his pants were shamelessly open, his thing hanging out, now gone limp all of a sudden. And the pleasurable feeling that he was just having was completely gone too; instead, he felt a clammy, squishy feeling down there. It was cold, cold as he had never felt before, but worse than that was the feeling of something wriggling inside there still. He jumped up at once, spraying his popcorn all over the place, and quickly zipping up, ran out of the hall.

"Where are you going, Anay?" he heard Shanaya ask him in an utterly shocked voice.

But he was out of the cinema hall already. The lobby was empty; all the screens were playing their respective movies. He ran all the way up to the nearest bathroom, and once there, he stood in front of the mirror and pulled up his shirt. The sight made him scream in horror.

Right from his navel to his groin, and creeping into the waistline of his boxers, were dozens of black fingermarks. They looked like scratches made all over his skin, but instead of being red with blood, they were made of some black, tarry substance. And he had that highly discomforting feeling that that was not all. Deep in there, he felt the cold clamminess of it all still. In terror, he slowly pulled his briefs down, and was beset with such nausea that made him faint. There, inside, on his inner thighs and—oh, Lord!—even on his penis, there was a deep black sludge. The goo dripped from him on the floor, and there was a copious amount of it, like he had been smeared profusely with that devil's bile. No, worse! It was as if someone had dipped their hands in it and fondled him. Over and over again. He rushed to the toilet, to wash away those infernal marks, shrieking, for there was now a freezing cold sensation down there that shot an ache up to his testicles, and then he realized—the pain wasn't just of the cold. Whatever had been sitting next to him in the dark movie hall had been trying to squeeze his manhood out of him.

Furiously, he threw water on himself, and cleaned whatever he could. The marks seemed to lighten, but he knew it would be a long time before they vanished. And he was in the toilet, locked inside, washing himself, when he was suddenly aware of the absolute silence the was around him, and then there was another hair-raising realization—that of a cold, cold breath falling upon the nape of his neck.

Did he dare turn behind and look?

No, he didn't.

For he knew what he would see—he would see the blazing blue eyes of the thing that was slowly taking him along to hell, and under those eyes, even in the absence of a mouth, there would be a wicked grin of triumph.

Pushing the door open as hard as he could, and nearly slipping on those slippery tiles, he ran out of that bathroom as fast as he could.